One Hot Summer

Wendi Hayman

Glory to Glory
Publications

Printed in the United States of America
First Printing, 2016
ISBN 978-0-9982435-1-1
Published by
Glory to Glory Publications, LLC
P.O. Box 855
Clayton, DE 19938
glorytoglorypublications@gmail.com
www.WendiHayman.com

Cover Design: Ed Wolfe at blazingcovers@gmail.com
Interior Book Design: www.TheLiarsCraft.com

Acknowledgements

    This book is dedicated to my husband, Tom Hayman, my girls, Marcia and Donye', my mother, my family and friends for believing in me and supporting me throughout the process. I thank Tom for being understanding of the long nights of writing, typing, and reading. Thank you for your encouragement and support. I thank Donye' for encouraging me and cheering me on. Thank you Marcia for being patient, understanding, putting up with my tantrums, but for being dedicated to this process with me and I thank your husband Lawrence for allowing me to borrow you for many long nights of editing.

    In 2012, God gave me the vision for this story but I said how I am going to write it because I never experienced molestation, and He told me it was somebody's story. In 2016 I learned who that somebody was and so the story of One Hot Summer was created. A special thank you goes to LaTanya Chance for being bold and brave enough to share your personal story with me and your testimony of overcoming and living in victory, and allowing me to use it as the foundation to write the story in the pages of this book.

    This book was written to expose the human truth of child molestation that has plagued so many homes and ruined the lives of many who have suffered in silence.

It was the day before Summer's 13th birthday, and she was finalizing everything for her birthday plans in New Orleans to celebrate with her best friend Charla, who shared the same birthday. Summer couldn't wait to go to New Orleans, Louisiana. She was surprised that her parents actually agreed to let her go. She checked her backpack once again to be sure that she had everything she would need for the trip; she didn't want to leave anything behind. Summer was so excited and nervous about the trip, and she hoped and prayed nothing would hinder the trip or her excitement about her birthday. Summer went to bed early that night because Charla and her mom, Ms. Charlotte, were picking her up at 7am for the 3-hour drive to New Orleans. Although Summer went to bed early, she couldn't fall asleep because of her excitement and anticipation for the trip.

Summer eventually drifted off to sleep, but was awakened shortly after. When she opened her eyes, Uncle Wil was standing over her with a big smile on his face. "Hey baby girl. Happy Birthday," he said holding out a wrapped gift box to Summer. Summer did what she did every time Uncle Wil showed up in her room; she stiffened her body. Summer should have known that she wasn't going to get a peaceful night of sleep tonight, but she was hopeful since tomorrow was her birthday. Uncle Wil kept trying to get Summer to take the gift, but she refused until he started to get agitated and smacked her in the face. With a tear coming out of her eye, Summer slowly reached for the gift. After what seemed like 30 minutes, Summer finally had all the wrapping off the box. She opened it and revealed a gold diamond heart necklace. Although the necklace was very beautiful, Summer refused to show any emotion to the gift because she knew it came with a very high price, the price of her 12-year-old innocence. Uncle Wil told Summer that she shined bright like a diamond and would always be in his heart. This was so untrue for Summer because ever since he's been coming to visit, her sparkle had dulled.

Summer used to be a happy little girl who absolutely loved to sing. She was also very artistic; she loved to draw, color, and paint. She drew pictures that were very bright, lively, and full of life, and she always sung as she did so. Unfortunately, Summer's spunky personality took a turn at 10 years old. Very unhappy in her home life, with both of her parents on drugs, crack to be exact, Summer longed for a change to her life. Their addiction to crack caused them to neglect her. At 12 years old, Summer was pretty much raising herself, and almost three years ago, she had been thrust into an aspect of adulthood that she was not ready for at such a young age.

One Hot Summer

Summer and her parents lived in a small 5-room home that consisted of two very small bedrooms, a tiny bathroom, a living room, and a kitchen in the small town of Natchez, Mississippi. Summer loved school because it got her away from her devastating home life. She absolutely hated for school to end, and she usually lingered around the playground as long as she could before going home. This had been her routine for quite some time. When Summer went home, she would go straight to her room to try to avoid her parents. She spent a lot of time in her room studying and reading books, and she ended her nights with drawing and singing to bring some joy her dull, dark world.

Summer was a very astute student and vowed to herself to always do her very best in school, not to please her parents but to secure her future for college. Summer badly wanted to excel in school so that when she got to high school in a few years, she would be able to get a full college scholarship and leave her destitute family home.

When Charla and her mom arrived the next day to pick up Summer for their trip, Summer was waiting at the door; she didn't even let Ms. Charlotte get out the car or let her parents know that she was leaving. Charla squealed in excitement as Summer jumped in the car. Summer tried to match Charla's excitement, but it was strained and forced. She was exhausted and still in pain from the torture she endured through the night. Thanks to the night she had Summer was no longer excited about her birthday but her anxiousness to go to New Orleans was still there.

As they got on the road to head to their destination, Summer immediately fell asleep. After Uncle Wil finally left, there was no way she could go back to bed, and she spent almost the rest of the night in the shower washing his filth off of her. Summer stayed in the shower until the water ran cold. When she eventually got out of the shower, she went back to her room and dressed. She then went into the front room and waited by the door until it was time for her to be picked up.

Once they arrived in New Orleans, they stopped for breakfast at Café Du Monde and had beignets and hot chocolate since it was still a little cool on this March 18th day. After breakfast, Ms. Charlotte took the girls to the Audubon Aquarium of the Americas. The girls really enjoyed seeing all of the different types of fishes. They had lunch at the Aquarium before heading to the Carousel Gardens Amusement Park. When they arrived at the amusement park, Summer looked around amazed at the vastness of the property and the amount of people. She knew that this would be the perfect place to set her plan in motion.

As time passed and it got later in the day, and Summer and Charla had played their hearts out and had ridden their tenth ride, Summer faked a stomach ache while they were in line for another ride. She begged Ms. Charlotte to let her go to the bathroom. After Ms. Charlotte hesitantly agreed, Summer ran off. She ducked into the bathroom, and after counting to 20, she snuck her head out to see where Ms. Charlotte's attention was. When she saw it wasn't in her direction, Summer quickly darted out of the restroom and rushed towards the direction of the park entrance. Summer walked quickly toward the entrance continuing to look back to be sure she wasn't being followed. She was able to sneak out of the amusement park without being caught. She quickly ducked into a nearby graveyard with large tombstones that she'd come upon. She walked swiftly through the graveyard until she got to about the middle where she hid behind a tombstone to breath. Summer was thankful that she was able to successfully execute her plan to run away during this day trip to New Orleans.

It had been 5 days since Summer got lost on purpose in New Orleans, and she was still hiding out in the cemetery. The snacks she packed had come to an end, and she was tired of sleeping outside. So, Summer wondered out of the cemetery and onto the streets of New Orleans. Summer had been walking for quite some time, not knowing the direction in which she was going, and she seemed to be heading into a not-so-pleasant looking neighborhood similar to the one she lived in back in Mississippi. Summer was walking slowly because she was very tired and weak from the lack of nourishment, and unknowingly, she walked up on a very tall, big, and husky man and a very skinny lady who were having an intense conversation. "Hey little girl, you're not from around here. What are you doing out on these streets?" she heard in a deep voice that boomed from the man. Summer stopped and stood frozen, afraid and not really sure if she should answer or run away. The man looked up from the little girl and scanned the streets to see if someone else was walking around who could have possibly been with the girl. The man, known on the streets as "Big Daddy," asked her again, "What are you doing out on these streets?" and when he reached out to grab Summer, she flinched then fell to the ground.

The man reached down and picked up the shaken little girl. "This girl looks like she been out on the street for a minute. Let's get her to the house," he told the woman. The man carried Summer in his arms to his Buick Regal and laid her down in the backseat. Summer quickly fell asleep on the supple leather seats.

When they arrived to the house where the man and woman lived, he scooped a sleeping Summer up into his arms and carried her into the house where he laid her down in the spare bedroom. Big Daddy assessed the girl and determined that she'd be asleep for some time, so he and the woman left her at the house and returned to the block where they came from. Big Daddy was a pimp who worked his main girl, Tess, and 6 other girls on the streets of Gentilly. When Big Daddy and Tess returned to the house later that night, they saw that the girl was still asleep.

The next day, Summer arose early and was frightened by not knowing where she was. She grabbed her backpack and timidly opened the door of the bright-yellow, sunflower decorated room that she slept in. She quietly crept out the bedroom door and down a hallway, which she assumed would lead to the front door, but the man was sitting in the front room of the house on a red, leather sofa reading the newspaper. When he heard the creak in the floor, Big Daddy lowered the paper and saw the girl trying to sneak out. "Girl, where you going? Go on in that kitchen and get you something to eat. I know you starving," Big Daddy said to

Summer while pushing his husky body up off the sofa. Tess heard the instruction, came out from the kitchen, and gently gestured for the girl to follow her. Summer shyly followed and sat down at the two-seated, quaint, wrought iron table adorned with a floral table cloth sitting in the center of the small kitchen. Although the kitchen was small, it was bigger than the kitchen in the home Summer left.

During the nourishing breakfast of thick cut bacon, sausage patties, eggs, and homemade biscuits, Big Daddy and Tess tried to learn why they found Summer on the streets of New Orleans alone, but they were only met with silence. The little girl looked like she'd suffered some type of trauma but would not speak up. They both asked probing questions, such as, "Did someone hurt you? Were you raped? Did you get put out? Did you runaway? Were you in an accident?" They inquired about her parents, any other family, and where she was from, but all the questions were answered with silence. They decided to back off after sensing that all the questions were causing the little girl some pain because of the tears streaming down her face and with her barely eating the food on her plate. They figured they would just wait and let the girl talk when she was good and ready.

Days after her strange arrival, Big Daddy and Tess took Summer shopping to buy her some clothes and any essentials she would need since she was going to remain with them for now. Big Daddy had been keeping his ear out on the street about a missing little girl, as well as asking questions, but he hadn't received any answers as of yet. So, they decided to let her stay with them since it didn't appear anyone was looking for her.

Summer was still withdrawn because of what she endured, so she still hadn't opened up to them. In her mind, Summer was very thankful to have been found by Big Daddy and Tess because she was tired of staying outside in the graveyard. While in the graveyard, Summer had to keep moving around at night because of drunkards, drug addicts, people having sex, and shootings. The last incident was a shooting in the daytime that mainly led Summer to escape the graveyard and roam the streets so she wouldn't be found by the police. She was sure that if the police found her they would send her back home to Natchez.

Although Big Daddy and Tess had been very kind and gentle to Summer, she was still cautious and in constant fear that something would happen to her. Even though she was no longer in her home, Summer kept having flashbacks of her abuse. She would be awakened from her sleep by the thoughts and images of the men kissing on her, touching her between her legs, and ultimately sticking their private part into hers and causing her much pain. She had many sleepless nights because of her nightmares.

Summer still remembered the first time it happened to her. Her mother and father came into her bedroom and sat down on the floor with her as she was drawing a picture of a swimming pool because she hoped to go swimming in the summer. They told her that they needed her to do a favor for them. Her parents told her that her dad's friend, whom she affectionately called Uncle Red, was coming over to see her, and they needed her to do whatever he asked her to do. Summer was 10 years old at the time, and she didn't understand what her parents were asking of her. Uncle Red was the first to take her innocence, but he never came back after that one time. Two other men came to the house and did the same thing to her that Uncle Red did, and they never came back either. For a long time, no other men came into Summer's room and made her do things she knew nothing about.

Even though it had stopped, Summer was already traumatized by the things her parents let these men do to her. For this, she despised her parents. She could not understand why they would put her through such a horrid thing. Everything about Summer changed, including her

9

mood, personality, and demeanor; she became extremely withdrawn and silent. She was no longer the bright and bubbly kid she had been. Summer's teacher even noticed the change in her, especially in her drawings that were now dark and scary pictures. When the teacher asked Summer if something was wrong, she responded, "No." Her mother always told her not to tell anyone what was going on at home because if she did, then no one would believe her, she would get her parents in trouble, and people would be mad at her if she got her parents in trouble. So, Summer kept silent and held everything in, suffering in silence. Her teacher had a conference with her mother about her change, but her mother lied and told the teacher that Summer was very saddened at the death of her pet. When Summer's teacher mentioned to her mom that she didn't know Summer even had a pet or ever mentioned that a pet died, her mother blew off the teacher comment.

One day, her parents came to her again asking for another favor. Summer cried in agony as her parents spoke. She begged and pleaded with them not the make her do it. She told them that she did not like what the men did to her, that it hurt her, and she didn't like how it made her feel. But her parents told her, "We really, really need you to help us out again." Summer would not agree, but her parents overrode her response and in walked her dad's best friend Uncle Wil. Uncle Wil was always so nice to Summer and would never cause her any harm, so Summer didn't think anything of it when he came into her room.

Uncle Wil talked with Summer for a little and asked her about the things she liked and what kind of toys she wanted. He told her that he would buy her anything she wanted. Summer smiled enthusiastically and said, "You will." She liked the sound of that promise, especially since her parents never bought her anything because they always said they didn't have enough money. There were days when they didn't even have anything to eat. Seeing that he'd said the right thing to Summer, he figured he had gained her trust.

"Let's play a game," he said to Summer.

She smiled and said, Okay." Since she was still a kid, Summer still liked to play games.

Wil said, "Let's see who's stronger, you or me."

"You're stronger Uncle Wil because you're bigger," Summer squealed in her child voice.

"Let's just see. You never know," Wil said until Summer agreed.

Wil laid his 5'7", skinny, 27-year-old body on the floor and told Summer to get on top of him and to hold his arms down. Doing as she was told Summer held him down, as she giggled Wil said, "See, you are strong Summer." Summer smiled and laughed in agreement. He then told her to lie down on the floor so he could see how strong he was. When he got up, Summer laid down in the space Wil was. He gently lay on top of her. Summer's eyes got big as she was familiar with this position.

"Uncle Wil, I don't want to play no more," she told him.

"It's ok sweetheart, you'll be ok," he assured her, but she wasn't believing it and squirmed under the weight of him as she started to cry out. Wil put a hand over her mouth, hushing her and telling her to relax, but Summer wouldn't stop. When he reached out to touch her under her prettiest sundress, the one her mother dressed her in, the same way the other men did, Summer cried in fear and shock. She could not believe that Uncle Wil wanted to hurt her just like the other men.

"Uncle Wil, I change my mind, I don't want any toys," Summer said to him hoping that would make him stop, but he just shushed her. Uncle Wil did just as the others did. He unbuckled his pants, pushed them down, pulled her panties off, and pushed himself inside of her. She lay under him and cried as he did his business. When he was done, he kissed her on the forehead, got up, and left. From that day forward, Uncle Wil would return multiple times a week for years. He kept his promise of buying her everything she wanted and would even occasionally take her out for ice cream and to the candy shop. Summer did like the fun outings, but she hated what she had to do in order to get them.

Ever since Summer arrived, Big Daddy kept Tess off the street to be there for the girl, and Tess was very thankful for that. Tess tried being loving toward Summer, but she wouldn't let her, despite how she frequently Tess tried to be. Due to her experiences with her own mother, Summer did not want any type of motherly nurturing.

Summer had been with Big Daddy and Tess for a month now, so she'd heard them say, and Big Daddy was now getting frustrated with the girl who didn't say anything and only stayed in the bedroom curled up on the bed. Tess was more patient with Summer, and she constantly reminded Big Daddy that the girl had obviously been traumatized and needed a little more time to warm up to them. Big Daddy's frustration went over the edge one day, and he told Tess that she couldn't stay home and baby sit the girl any longer. "It's time for you to go back to work." Tess became distraught because she was really tired of working the streets for Big Daddy, and she saw the girl being there as her way out. She'd been working for Big Daddy since she was 22 years old, and now at 38, her body had grown tired and weary from 16 years of meeting the sexual needs of johns.

Tess had always wanted a child, but every time she became pregnant, Big Daddy would either make her get an abortion or beat her until she ended up having a miscarriage. So having this beautiful, although sad, little girl was just what Tess longed for. Later that evening, Big Daddy came back to the house to get Tess to go to work. Tess and Summer were in Summer's room, and Tess was reading a book to Summer. The girl sat quietly and listened as Tess read *The Jungle Book.* Not knowing the girl's age, Tess just bought a few children's books for them to read together. Big Daddy came through the door and yelled for Tess to get dressed because it was time for her to hit the streets. Tess silently got up. She had already been fighting with Big Daddy against him putting her back to work; she was tired of fighting, and she especially didn't want to fight in front of the girl.

As Tess was leaving out the door behind Big Daddy, Summer quickly jumped from the bed, cried out, "No," and grabbed a hold of her leg begging her not to leave. That action stopped Tess and Big Daddy in their tracks since it was the very first time they heard anything from the girl besides silent crying at night. Tess quickly turned around and embraced Summer, which she immediately welcomed. It felt so good to Tess since this was the first time the girl allowed her to be touched or shown any affection. Seeing the sight infuriated Big Daddy because he really needed to get Tess back on the street because she was his biggest money maker. But at the same time, actually seeing the girl's tears softened his stance.

Finally, she spoke. "My name is Summer and I am 13 years old," she said just slightly above a whisper. "It is so nice to meet you Summer and to finally know your name," Tess responded kneeling on the floor face to face with Summer. Summer then reached her hand out to Big Daddy to shake his and spoke a soft, "Hi." Big Daddy then completely melted from a block of ice into a water puddle as he looked into the girl's hazel-colored eyes. Summer always kept her head hung low, and her eyes cast downward, so neither he nor Tess ever saw their beautiful hue.

Since Summer had finally spoken, Big Daddy decided to let Tess stay in, and he stayed in too. He put a call in to all the other girls and told them he'll collect in the morning. At that point, they were all in the room sitting on the bed as Summer began to open up and tell them who she was.

3

Big Daddy jumped up off the bed furious while Tess just sat totally stunned at the things that were coming from this little girl's mouth. They could not believe that she was actually 13 years old and had gone through so much at such a young age. She had a small frame and child-like demeanor, and she looked like she could have easily passed for 6 or 7 years old. Big Daddy slammed his fist hard on the dresser; he could not believe the parents of this little girl had been selling her for drugs since she was 10 years old. Big Daddy paced the floor in anger. He wanted to jump in his car right then and there and drive to Natchez, Mississippi to beat the life out of the girl's parents. And to think that perverted men even had the nerve to have sex with her the day before her birthday. It's no wonder the girl ran away from home. Big Daddy was glad that she was smart enough to come up with a plan to get out of such a treacherous household.

Tess continued to sit quietly as the girl's story touched her deeply. Tess too was molested as a child by a grown man. She was much younger than Summer, only 8 years old, when she was molested by her mother's boyfriend. Her life's struggles eventually led to the life she was living now as a prostitute as a result of low self-esteem and rejection. Big Daddy didn't know any of this. When Big Daddy met Tess, she was struggling to survive and was bouncing around from guy to guy, many who were abusive. Big Daddy took her in and promised her a stable life, which he has provided, but she had to work for it.

When Tess had gotten molested, she didn't do as her molester said and not tell anyone. She immediately ran and told her mother what happened to her, which turned out to be a big mistake. Tess was totally stunned at what came from her 24-year-old mother's mouth when she cried out to her about what had happened. Tess's mother said five simple but disheartening words that she'd never forget: "I knew you wanted him." How could a mother actually tell her child that she wanted a grown man?

Tess had been sitting on the floor in her bedroom playing with her Barbie dolls. She was pretending that the best friend dolls were going shopping when John, her mother's boyfriend, came in and silently closed the door behind him. He squatted down on the floor with Tess and she didn't think anything of it. He asked her, "What are the dolls doing?" She told him "Shopping" in her child tone of voice and continued playing. "That's funny that you're playing shopping and your mom has just gone shopping," John told Tess. Tess briefly paused because her mom had never left her home alone, especially not with a man, and she immediately became uncomfortable. John picked up two dolls and played along, which quickly started to relax the

and he pushed himself into her mouth." Tess cried through the motions he made her do. He was also making funny noises. John then picked Tess up with one hand, with his other hand on himself, and threw her onto the bed. She rolled over trying to get away, but he pinned her down and laid himself atop of her small child frame. What he did next caused Tess excruciating pain in her private area and in her little mind. As he got up, he pulled his pants up while Tess lay on the bed curled up in a ball crying. John told her, "And you better not tell anybody. But nobody is going to believe you anyway," then arrogantly left her room.

Tess's mom returned home about an hour later and peeked in on her in her room. She found Tess curled up in a corner crying. When her mom came over to ask her what was wrong, she told her mom that John had touched her in her private area and hurt her there. She told her mom that he made her touch him too, and she didn't like it. Tess's mom immediately jumped up yelling at her saying, "I knew you wanted him! Always on his lap watching TV and laying on him." A young Tess defended herself asking her mom what she meant by that. Tess cried and pleaded with her mom telling her that her private area hurt really badly, and her mom immediately threw back, "You're going to hurt somewhere else because I'm about to beat your tail, wearing that little bitty romper around my boyfriend." She snatched her belt out of the loops on her jeans and went to beating Tess. Tess screamed and cried, begging and pleading with her mother to stop. Tess simply did not understand what she did wrong. This man hurt her, and her mom was beating her for it. Tess just knew her mother would believe her, but John was right instead.

After her mom finished beating her, she went into the bathroom and drew the hottest bathwater to throw Tess in, so she could scold her "fast tail." She called Tess to the bathroom, shoved her into the tub of scolding hot water, and told her to scrub herself good; Tess did so for a very long time. She was trying to scrub away every touch, every kiss, and more importantly, the pain that was left in-between her legs. Tess had no idea how to comprehend what happened to her; her 8-year-old mind just could not process it.

The next day, while Tess's mom's girlfriends were over, she told them what happened, and they too scolded Tess. They said that they would definitely keep their kids away from her "fast, hot in the pants behind." This hurt Tess so much. Tess asked her mom if she could walk down to her grandmother's house, and she said yes. "You better not stop at any boy's house along the way," her mother scolded. Tess looked at her mom with a look of confusion on her face, she never told her this before when she walked downed to her grandmother's. Once out the door, Tess took off running down the street to her grandmother's house, only 3 houses down, crying just as hard as she was running. When she reached the porch, she was out of breath and heaving hard, but she still managed to bang on the door to get her grandmother's attention. Once inside, Tess's grandmother noticed how distraught her only grandchild was and immediately went into alarm mode. Through the storm of tears pouring from her eyes, Tess recanted the details of yesterday and today to her grandmother. Nana, as Tess affectionately called her grandmother, jumped up from her place on the couch, went into her bedroom, and grabbed her pistol. She told Tess, "Child wait here, I'll be right back," and stormed out the door.

Tess had no idea what transpired down at her mother's house, but after a long time, her grandmother came back into the house carrying a suitcase that contained all of Tess's clothes and as many toys as she could fit in there. She told Tess that she was never going back to that house as long as she was alive. Tess was thankful for her Nana and lived with her until she was 17 years old. Her Nana died shortly thereafter. Since it was several months until her 18th birthday, New Orleans Child Protective Services would not allow her to live alone, so Tess had to live in foster care until she turned 18.

Tess was moved to tears not just for the hurt she felt for Summer, but also because the pain that she thought was deeply suppressed seemed to have reared its ugly head. But Tess couldn't allow this to affect her. She had to remain strong for this little girl who has come into her life for some unknown reason. Tess was using all her strength to bear the work that she had been doing for the past 16 years. Tess's body had taken a beaten both physically and sexually over the years. Due to her good genes, she was able to maintain her shapely figure on her 5'7" slender frame and her beautiful, smooth Mocha complexion skin. Tess's eyes were a natural brown color. Over the years, they appeared to have turned as dark as coal due the darkness that resided deep within the crevices of her soul. One thing Big Daddy required was that she kept up her breathtakingly beautiful appearance. Her beauty is what drew the customers, and it was her sexual performance that kept them coming back.

Sobering up from her own pain that she'd carried for years towards her mother, her abusers, and especially towards Big Daddy, Tess embraced Summer and whispered a prayer of thanks in her heart. Something within her told Tess that this little girl was the answer to the prayer she had been saying for years, which was to be delivered from the streets and the brutal life of prostitution. She and Big Daddy would only go to church on Christmas, Easter, and maybe the occasional Sunday because he believed that going every now and then would cleanse his soul from the demons of the streets. Tess used those opportunities to cry out to God to save her.

Seeing how distraught Summer was, Big Daddy decided that it was best she not be left alone, so he told Tess that she could stay with the girl until he could find a sufficient baby sitter. Tess was very thankful for the rest that her body would be able to get, even if it was only for a short period. This was upsetting Big Daddy because Summer and Tess were messing up his money. When customers noticed that Tess was off the street, they would often turn away, and they were not easily accepting of Big Daddy's other girls. He had to do a lot of begging and pleading to some customers who would try to leave after their request for Tess could not be fulfilled. Big Daddy felt that all this begging was making him look like a little punk trick.

Since Summer would now be living with Tess and Big Daddy, he had to find something for her to do because she couldn't go to school since she was a runaway. So Big

Daddy drove down the street to talk to old lady Mrs. Robertson, who was an educator who lived in his neighborhood. He discussed paying her to home school Summer, and Mrs. Robertson happily agreed to the time and of course the sum Big Daddy offered. Big Daddy had plans for Summer when she got older, but he doesn't employ dummies. Most of Big Daddy's girls came from destitute situations, but many were attractive, clever, and street savvy. He wanted to assure Summer had the same potential.

Mrs. Robertson, a 72-year-old retired widower, worked with Summer 3 hours each day. While Summer was at Mrs. Robertson's, Tess was working on the streets. When Big Daddy picked up Summer after her home schooling, she would ride around with him learning the street business. Big Daddy would teach her all that she needed to know to be tough on these streets, especially when she would start interacting with the hoodlums, both male and female. Although Summer didn't understand what she was being taught at the time, she continued to take in the information. Summer had really warmed up to Big Daddy because she saw that he was not one to hurt her. He was a strong protector of her, which was something that she did not get from her own father. Her father threw her to the wolves and sold her body for a temporary high.

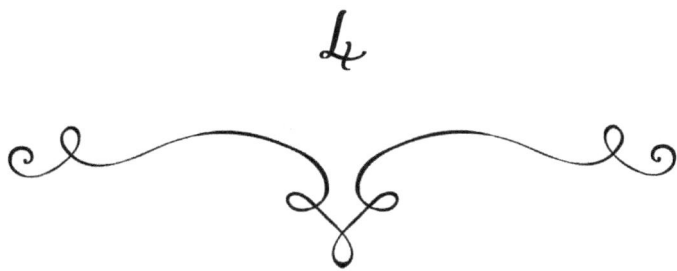

As she grew older, Summer started to develop more into her looks and body. Although she was a scrawny kid, she was nicely developed in her bust and butt. Big Daddy always had plans for her after she first came to them and seeing how nicely she was looking and developing, he was now ready to put his plans into action.

Summer was now a tough fighter who could hold her own thanks to Big Daddy. She wasn't as much of the shy, withdrawn, introvert that she used to be, but she did like to be alone and usually stayed to herself. Summer had gotten into too many fights to count with neighborhood kids when she hung out at the park and other areas of the streets. She had to fight girls because they bullied her for her small frame and her good looks. Summer was light-skinned with cheeks full of freckles. But her hazel eyes and reddish-brown, long wavy hair were her best features, which caused the other girls to dislike her. Her frame was small because she didn't eat much, but she did inherit the shape of a black girl, with her hips and round behind telling a different story of her heritage.

She had been very uncomfortable around other people. The teens would try to get her to talk, but anxiety would paralyze her and most often she'd leave the park. So when the other girls tried to hang around her, she would reject them. They thought she was "dissing" them because she thought she was cute "cause she had light skin with pretty eyes" or because she was better than then them, but neither was the case.

She also had to fight off boys who crossed the line with her or tried to take advantage of her because of her shyness. They took her introvert personality as being gullible but little did they know who she belonged to. There were a couple of times where Summer had to bring Big Daddy to the park to defend her. After learning that Big Daddy was her guardian, no one messed with Summer in a bullying way again although they still picked on and teased her.

Summer did take an interest in one boy who she'd met at the park. She met him one day while she was sitting alone under a tree doodling in her notebook. Since Summer didn't trust anyone other than Big Daddy and Tess, she would not engage in any conversation he was trying to have with her. But every time he saw her around in the park, he would say something to her. He was nice looking to Summer with his milk chocolate skin, deep-set brown eyes, black wavy hair, and muscular frame standing around 5'10". Summer silently enjoyed his attention, but she did not know how to interact with others, especially males. Since he would speak to her every time he saw her, Summer now looked forward to going out for quiet time in the park just to see the cute guy.

The mean girls would still come and pick on her. Even after she would change locations in the park, they would always find her, but Summer would never engage them. She hadn't seen the nice guy in the park for a couple of days, and it disappointed her. One day, a group of four girls were really picking on her. One of them grabbed her right foot, snatched off the Gucci sneaker she was wearing, and started tossing it around with the others. Summer jumped up and chased them back and forth trying to get her shoe back. After numerous attempts of chasing the girls around trying to get her shoe back, the nice guy came out of nowhere and grabbed the girl with the shoe by the waist, took it from her, and shooed all of them away. They were mad at him and started to cuss him out.

He walked over to Summer, who was out of breath, and handed her shoe back to her. "Here you go," he said.

Summer let out a breathless, "Thank you," took her shoe, and bent over to put it back on.

"Wow, so she does have a voice," he let out in a laugh. Summer even laughed at that.

"And she laughs too," he responded. "Today must be my lucky day."

"Everyone calls me Kai," he said, formally introducing himself to Summer.

"Hi, Kai. I'm Summer," she responded shyly.

"Summer, huh," Kai responded. "You look more like Sunshine." Summer put her head down and smiled shyly; this was her first time ever receiving such a compliment.

25

"Let me walk you back to your spot," he told her, and Summer followed right along beside him and listened as he talked.

He stayed with her for a little while under the tree once they got back to her spot. She learned that Kai's real name was Mikaiel. After that day, whenever she would go to the park, she would look for Kai. If she didn't see him, she would be disappointed, but eventually, he would come and find her. One time, he came to her house looking for her when he couldn't locate her in the park. When she asked him how he knew where she lived, he told her that one day he kept a close eye on her as she walked home so he would know which house she lived in.

Summer began to hang out with Kai whenever she could, and they would often hang out well into the night. Kai was a young dude from the projects who had aspirations of being a rapper, but until then, he was doing a little slanging to put money in his pocket and keep food on the table for him and his 5 siblings. Kai's mom was put in a mental institution after she'd suffered a psychotic breakdown from a beating she'd taken from the hands of her youngest child's father. Since Kai was 21, the state let him keep his younger siblings instead of putting them into the foster care system. He had gotten a job at a McDonald's to show proof of employment, and his 18-year-old sister would babysit his younger brothers ages 10, 8, and 3. Once his guardianship application was approved, he quickly quit his job and got back on the streets. Summer learned all of this during their late night hangouts at the park while he was working his spot. Although Summer had gotten comfortable

26

with Kai, she wasn't comfortable enough to tell him her real story, so she told him that Big Daddy was her real father and that her mom sent her to live with him at 14 when she could no longer handle her teenage behavior.

The day Big Daddy found out about Kai, he questioned Summer, and she told him that she liked Kai and liked hanging out with him, but that was it. Big Daddy was all about business and didn't believe in giving away free goods, but he said the only reason he would allow her to be with the boy was because it would give her practice for the work she was going to do. But Summer wasn't interested in Kai sexually, and he didn't press her about it either.

Summer knew that she couldn't get too comfortable being a teenager and hang out with the neighborhood teens because Big Daddy had told her so. "It's time for you to take care of grown folks business" he reminded her. Now at 18 years old and finished with her home schooling, Big Daddy was ready to put Summer to work. He and Tess fought about this for years, but this is what Big Daddy planned all along. Big Daddy reminded Tess that she'd been asking to get off the streets for years, and this was her only way out, no alternative. Besides, it was time for Summer to work for her keep. Although they had gotten her an illegal ID card, she couldn't get a legitimate job because she didn't have the proper documentation.

Big Daddy was excited to add this "young tender," an unused product, to his collection of girls. His goal was to use Summer to draw in young customers in their twenties and thirties because most of his customers were much older. However, he knew all the old perverts would be coming out as soon as they saw this young girl on the streets. Tess had already taken Summer shopping for street working clothes, she taught her how to drink alcohol, and she gave her some pain numbing drugs, which she would need to numb herself from the emotional pain that was sure to follow. The stories Tess told Summer scared her tremendously, but she knew that there was no backing down.

Summer was not looking forward to going to work on the streets even though she had been taught and shown the business, and she knew it inside and out. She knew she had to do what she had to do to survive in Big Daddy's house. Big Daddy had been training her in the streets for when this time came. He told her during her many training drive thru's that when she turned 18, he would be putting her to work. He also threatened her at the same time that if she tried to run away, he would find her and kill her, especially after all he had done to give her a good, stable life and make sure that she had the best of everything. Though Big Daddy was pretty soft and sensitive with her, she believed his threat and dared not cross him, no matter the cost for her life.

The price for Summer was much higher than it was for Tess and the other girls. The customers complained of such once Summer was presented to them, but Big Daddy explained to the customers that they were getting new, young, fresh merchandise. At first, there were complaints and many turn downs because of Summer's scrawny body, but eventually after much coercing, there were takers. Once business had taken off for Summer, and men had gotten their first taste of the young girl, they were hooked and came back continuously and often for more. Many of the early customers were exactly what Big Daddy wanted, young street dealers who weren't afraid to spend money for a woman's goods.

With Tess still off the street, Big Daddy had finally scored one of Tess's regular customers for Summer. He was a much older man with plenty of money to spend. Big Daddy convinced him to give Summer a try one day when Tess wasn't working. Summer got into the car with the customer not knowing much about who the guy was. When she saw he was much older, there was an immediate trigger. She suddenly had a flashback to her past, which made her lash out at the older man. She started screaming, cussing, and fighting the man while calling him a nasty old pervert who preyed on children for sex. Since the car hadn't moved from the pickup spot, Big Daddy heard the commotion. When he saw she was in a fit of rage, he rushed over to stop her. When he reached the car and looked into her eyes, he saw a different Summer then the one he knew. Big Daddy yanked her from the car and asked what was going on. She told him that when she looked at that old man, she saw the face of every abuser who molested her. She realized that she had been suppressing her emotions and that man brought out everything she was trying to hide from.

Big Daddy took Summer off the streets for a couple of days to allow her time to calm down from the two-year-old kind of temper tantrum she had, but he also knew she needed some settling in her emotions. He understood what she went through as a child, and it burned him up, but she was no longer a child. She was a big girl, and it was now time for her to live like it.

5

Following the first outburst, the working periods with Summer no longer went so well. She would have bursts of anger and rage that would come intermittently whenever she was with an older customer. She jumped on one customer in the hotel and beat him to the point where he had to go to the hospital. Big Daddy was not having this, and he wasn't going to have this little girl mess up his business or his money. So he began to beat on her. He told her that he was going to beat that anger and rage out of her. Summer couldn't believe that Big Daddy had turned on her. Summer hurt so badly after that beating; she hurt more emotionally than she did physically. There were times where he fussed or yelled at her, but for the most part, Big Daddy never laid a hand on her. He was usually really soft and sensitive toward Summer. Big Daddy's anger with Summer had gotten to the point where she and Tess began to talk of plans to run away because Tess didn't want Summer to get caught in the same lifecycle as she had for as long as she did.

Summer was young and could have a bright future if she got to the right place in life.

During her time off, Summer spent more time with Kai. She'd gotten really comfortable with him, and she even allowed him to have sex with her. Sex with Kai was very different than with the customers. It actually made her have feelings in her body that she'd never felt before. He was very gentle and passionate with her, and he took his time with every stroke. The customers she was with were always going fast and rushed, and she was very disinterested in them. Summer and Kai had sex often, and she really enjoyed being with him. She was starting to feel like she was falling in love.

Summer and Kai would hang out at the park, and she was even brave enough to go to his apartment in the projects. He even took her the movies one day. Kai made her feel really good. He made her feel special, gave her compliments all time, and made her feel like a person. Summer was so smitten with Kai that she never wanted to leave him when it was time to go, and she definitely didn't want to go back to work on the streets.

Eventually, Big Daddy himself had to come up with a plan to help Summer channel her anger in another way. He never thought that putting Summer to work on the streets would trigger old emotional wounds from her childhood, but he had no other choice because she had to work. One day, he decided to take her to the gun range to see if that would help. He told her to see the face of every one of her abusers that she could remember on the target, and when she did that, Summer blasted the targets. She did exceptionally well for her first time, however, anger directed in the right place can be good and bad. Firing the gun was exhilarating to Summer. Big Daddy would then bring Summer back to the gun range several times a month to let her exert some anger.

When Big Daddy felt like she was at the stage where the initial shock of the streets was over for Summer, he quickly put her back to work. Big Daddy also put an end to her time with Kai, and this devastated Summer. She went back to work begrudgingly, but there was also something different about her. She had a new level of confidence and a new swag. She now welcomed her customer's advances and no longer fought them. No, she didn't want to have sex with these men, especially the older ones, but there was something that was driving her to perform sexually as if she was ok with the act. Sex with Kai awakened something in her. This drive caused Summer to develop an unusual and uncanny relationship with her customers, kind of like she'd cast a spell on them. She still had a few outbursts from time to time but nothing major or alarming. Big Daddy wished he could put the girl on some crazy medicine to calm her down, but he was enjoying the money she was making. Taking her to the gun range seemed to have worked because the outbursts of rage with his customers subsided. Business was now good and had been going well for a couple of years.

Years later, Big Daddy sat down with Summer to construct a plan for her to go back to Natchez, Mississippi and execute a plan of revenge against her abuser Wil. It was coming up to Summer's 21st birthday, and he thought it would be a good idea if she returned to her hometown to come face to face with him now that she was old enough to confront him. In all the years she'd been in New Orleans, Summer hadn't even thought about returning to that place in the 8 years she had been gone. Summer did all that she could to suppress the memories of her childhood. As she got older, she no longer thought of her parents who were the source of her pain due to their addiction to crack. Big Daddy and Tess had become her parents. There were no pleasant memories that came to mind for Summer at the mention of Natchez. Summer had constructed a new mindset, new thoughts, new memories, and a new life for herself here in New Orleans. The trickling thoughts of Natchez began to cause her some distress. Summer no longer remembered all of her abusers because most of them only happened once, but she did remember the one whose sexual abuse was regular up until her 13th birthday.

Timothy Wilks, known as Timmy, and Wilburn Thibodeaux, known as Wil, were best friends and kind of like brothers ever since grade school. After graduating high school, Timmy could only get a job as a mechanic because he barely made it through high school. Wil, on the other hand, was good at math and loved working with numbers, and he graduated top of their class in 1985. After graduation, he secured a job at a local accounting firm in Jackson, Mississippi where he worked through the summer until he started the undergraduate Accounting program on full academic scholarship at Alcorn State University. Wil worked at the accounting firm every summer during college saving up all of his money.

Upon graduation and completing his final summer with the firm, Wil returned home to Natchez where he opened his own tax & accounting office. He rented a small office on the main street of S. Canal in the center of town. The office only had enough room for two small desks for him and a secretary. Wil had big dreams for his tax & accounting firm. There weren't any in Natchez at the time. Up until that point, the town folks and business owners would go to other towns, or they would have to get their taxes done by the Business professors at Alcorn University. So, Wil's dream was to open and operate a successful tax & accounting firm in Natchez to service the current businesses and the future businesses of Natchez, which he knew were to come.

At first, business started off a little bit slow, but eventually word spread around town about how proficient Wil was in tax laws after the first tax season of him being in business. After word spread about how he saved the owners of a small dealership/auto mechanic shop a lot on their taxes and how a few people got good tax refunds, business began to pick up quickly and had grown ever since. Wil got to the point where in just 3 short years, he was expanding his business and added two Alcorn University business students as interns. Wil was doing well professionally and financially.

Things weren't going so well for Timmy. He was having difficulty keeping a job, and he was stressed out because he couldn't care for his wife and 8-year-old daughter. He and his long-time girlfriend Bernadette "Bernie" Wilks got married right out of high school since she was pregnant during their senior year. Timmy always had to borrow money from family, friends, and especially Wil when he was in between jobs. Then Timmy finally got a job at the fabrication plant, but after 2 years of being there, things took a sudden turn. He started coming to work late, and when he showed up, he would fall asleep on the job. No one knew what happened to Timmy or why the sudden change in behavior. After the company had a random drug test due to his suspicious behavior, he tested positive for the new street drug, crack cocaine, which got him fired immediately.

Bernie worked as a clerk at the local library. She was a very smart girl but had turned down going to college when she found out that she was pregnant at the end of her senior year, and she didn't want to leave Timmy. The two of them were inseparable ever since they met freshman year of high school. Bernie loved books and loved to read, so working at the library was a dream job for her. When she found out Timmy was fired from his good job at the plant, she was devastated because things had been going so well for them. They had purchased a small, although slightly desolate, quaint house that was perfect for their small family. Timmy didn't tell Bernie that the real reason he lost his job was for drugs; he told her it was because he made an error on the assembly line.

Things got really tough for their family trying to make it on Bernie's small clerk salary and the food stamps they were getting, but when money started coming up missing and she was unable to pay some bills, Bernie became very angry. She would confront Timmy about the missing money, but he would always make up some lame excuse and then charm her like he always could. Bernie was so in love with Timmy that she believed anything he told her, but she started having suspicions that Timmy was cheating on her with another woman. Although Timmy mainly stayed home all day drinking alcohol, he exhibited strange behavior and would go missing at night after she'd gone to bed. One day, Bernie came home early after the school called her at work because Summer had gotten sick at school, and the school couldn't reach Timmy because the phone was cut off for non-payment of the bill.

When they arrived to the house, Bernie put her daughter in the bed and immediately went to find Timmy. When she went in her bedroom, she was shocked at what she saw. Timmy was sprawled out on the bed naked with another woman draped over him, and they were both knocked out sleep. What was even more shocking was the crack pipe in-between them. Bernie threw a fit, waking them both up. They got up, the woman dressed quickly, and attempted to run out of the room. But she wasn't fast enough. Bernie snatched her by her long locks of matted black hair and gave her a beat down for being in her house and screwing her husband. The skinny white chick was eventually able to break away from the scuffle and quickly ran out of the house.

Too high to comprehend all that was going on, Timmy just sat up on the side of the bed not wanting to ruin his high. But he sobered up quickly when Bernie started yelling and screaming at him as she proceeded to strike him in his face and chest with her open palms. He retaliated back with one hard strike to her face that caused Bernie to fall over the other side of their twin-sized bed. Bernie just lay on the floor crying from the devastation of the scene that just unfolded in her life. Bernie was more hurt from the fact that Timmy just hit her, which was something he had never done before even when he was drunk. Timmy quickly dressed himself and left the house in a rage.

Later that evening when Timmy returned home, he was quiet and surprisingly sober. He didn't even go grab a drink like he normally would have. That was mainly because he didn't have any money. His M. O. was always to take some money out of Bernie's purse for a drink or drugs, but he didn't even think about doing that. This time he needed a clear head for the talk he needed to have with Bernie. He needed her to understand that he was sorry for being with another woman but, more importantly, for hitting her. When they talked, Timmy was very apologetic, and Bernie could tell that he was sincere, especially since he was sober for the first time in a long time. Timmy went on to explain that he had been doing drugs for a couple of years now, which was the reason he had gotten fired from the plant in the first place. He further explained that getting high alone wasn't much fun, and when he met Kat, another customer of his dealer, he didn't think it would be an issue of them getting high together. Thought he never expected for them to have sex.

Bernie was beyond shattered; she was downright mad and angry, but she loved Timmy with every fiber of her being. Sobbing, she asked him if he had any more crack, and he told her no because he and Kat smoked it all. Thinking that she was going to ask him to stop, Timmy was prepared to make up excuses, but Bernie got up and walked towards their bedroom. She returned to the living room with money in hand and told him to go and buy some more. Timmy was stunned and thankful at the same time. He jumped up off the battered couch and rushed out of the house not thinking once to ask Bernie why she wanted him go and buy some crack.

When Timmy returned moments later, Bernie was waiting for him in the bedroom where she had changed the sheets and cleaned the bedroom of the filth from another woman. When he sat down, she asked him to show her the crack, and he did. Bernie examined the two tiny rocks rolled in Saran Wrap. She then said, "Let me see you smoke it." Timmy was all too eager to take a hit because he really needed a high after his last one was blown from all the chaos that went on earlier. Bernie had heard about crack cocaine, how it caused a serious addiction, its ramifications on the body, and what it does to a person's mental capacity. But at that moment, all she thought about was her love for Timmy and how she would do anything to keep him, especially to keep him out of the arms of another woman. Bernie thought back briefly to how she used to steal money, food, and cigarettes for Timmy throughout their high school years. Timmy and Bernie understood one another; they were inseparable, and they'd gotten into a lot of mischief together.

After she saw Timmy was finished, Bernie reached for his pipe to do what she saw him do. But as quickly as she put her lips around the neck of the pipe, Timmy snatched it from her in a panic asking, "What are you doing?" Bernie said, "I want to be the only woman who you ever sleep with, and if that means you need someone to get high with too, I'm going to do that as well." She expressed her deepest love for Timmy by kissing him deeply and told him how she loved him more than she loved herself. Timmy explained to Bernie that she was too smart and intelligent to get mixed up with drugs, and that it was bad enough she was with a broke, busted, drug addict like himself. Bernie wouldn't hear it. She said, "If it's good enough for you, then as your wife, I will get high too if getting high with you is going to keep us together." All Bernie wanted was for her and Timmy to be together by any means necessary. With that being said, she gently grabbed the pipe from his grips, put her lips around it, closed her eyes, and inhaled the vapors.

6

Big Daddy, Tess, and Summer came up with the plan for her return to Natchez. This actually scared Summer because she didn't remember much about Natchez, and she wouldn't know the first place to go. All she remembered was her parents' names, Timmy and Bernie, who she definitely didn't want to see. Just the thought of her parents' names caused Summer to tremble, and she became visibly shaken. Seeing what was taking place, Tess spoke up and said that she should go along with Summer to Mississippi for comfort and support, but Big Daddy immediately dismissed her suggestion. He needed her on her post more now that Summer would be gone, which would take away from his money.

Summer thought the plan they'd come up with was a good idea, but it actually scared her. She'd never thought she'd do something like Big Daddy had suggested. She really wished she could talk to Kai about it and get his advice, but since she didn't tell him the truth about who she was, that was out of the picture. Besides, Kai was now locked up for getting caught selling drugs, and she couldn't talk to him until he called her collect. A jealous kid snitched on Kai and set him up with the cops, so Kai was doing an 8-month sentence in the city jail since it was his first charge of possession.

The day finally came for Summer to take the trip to Natchez. Big Daddy had secured her a fake driver's license, a car registered in her name, and car insurance. He had to make sure everything was air tight as not to raise any suspicions while she made the trip. Although the trip to Natchez was only a short, 3-hour ride, he didn't want anything to happen along the way. Big Daddy bought a Toyota Corolla, which was a small car that would be inconspicuous enough not to draw any attention from highway patrol, especially since Summer would be carrying the Glock 42 .380 pistol he bought her for her 21st birthday.

Summer couldn't sleep at all the night before. She had become tough and fearless, but the thought of returning to the place of her nightmarish childhood scared the crap out of Summer, literally. Summer had been to the bathroom three times that night. It was coming out of her as if demons were leaving her body. Summer was a nervous wreck. She had been planning this moment for weeks, and her anticipation for the trip was all built up. But why was she now at the point of backing out? Summer's nerves were bad for a number of reasons. She feared that going back to Natchez would bring back all the bad memories. She feared facing her parents and what they might do to her when they saw her. Although she wished they were all dead, she feared coming face to face again with her molesters, especially Uncle Wil, who she wanted most badly to suffer for the wrong he'd done to her. He continuously raped her of her innocence, her youth, her childhood, and no telling what else as he molested her week after week for almost 3 years for his own filthy self-gratification and the selfishness of her crackhead parents. Summer was scheduled to leave around noon, but since she didn't get much sleep, she didn't leave until after 1 o'clock that afternoon.

The short, 3-hour drive to Natchez seemed to take Summer forever. She tried to maintain a steady pace during the 60 mph speed limit on I-10 W and then when she got on US-61 entering Mississippi, but it seemed like her car was going no faster than 30 mph. Her thoughts and heart were moving faster than her car. As she approached the sign that read *Welcome to Historic Natchez on the Mississippi*, Summer's heart began to race even more. When she approached the Visitor's Center, she immediately pulled her car into the parking lot. Summer jumped out of her car, ran to the ladies room, and immediately threw up when she entered the restroom stall. After she came out of the stall and rinsed her face and mouth in the sink, she looked in the mirror and saw that her already light complexion looked flushed. Summer leaned over the sink in anguish. After gathering herself, Summer walked out of the restroom, went back to her car, got in, and sat for a few moments before driving off. When she entered the small town through the main road, she immediately realized that nothing looked familiar although she'd taken many trips to town with her mother.

Tess tried to feed her a nice breakfast before she left, but Summer's nerves wouldn't allow her to eat. She tried to nibble on the small snacks she packed as she listened to her new Usher CD to keep her mind occupied, but nothing worked; her thoughts just ran rampant. After driving about 3 miles into town, Summer saw the sign for a diner and pulled into its parking lot. The car was good on gas, and she still had over ¼ tank left from her fill up the night before. Summer opened the door and stepped out onto the gravel parking lot in her Gucci flip flops. This made her wish she'd worn her Gucci sneakers instead. One thing she enjoyed about the business with Big Daddy was that he lets her and Tess wear the finest designer labels. He would regularly take them on shopping trips to the Riverwalk and Shops at Canal, and he also allowed them to shop online. They had the top names in designer clothes, shoes, handbags, and accessories.

After stepping out of the car, she pulled down what she could of her thigh high Polo shorts. She stretched her whole body then leaned back into the car to grab her black Gucci cross body handbag and draped it across her. Summer walked steadily to the entrance of the *Eat in Route* diner. When she pulled the door open, the chime signaling her arrival caused Summer to jump and make her heart pound. The sound was very familiar, but she couldn't quite gather her thoughts as to where she'd heard it before. Summer was greeted by a short and petite girl, who looked to still be in high school. She was sat at a booth immediately. While perusing the menu, a waitress, whose name tag read Melinda, came to greet her. She politely greeted Summer and took her drink order. Summer ordered a Coke, her favorite drink. When Melinda returned with the soda pop, Summer placed her order for a chicken club sandwich with no cheese, the bacon to be cooked crispy, on wheat toast without butter, and fries. Melinda rushed off to place the new customer's order, but not without looking back at the young lady a few times. Her face was beautiful, but she looked strikingly familiar.

The diner was no longer busy now that they had passed the afternoon rush of the lunch crowd, so Melinda stood for a moment trying to figure out who the young lady could be. Melinda returned with her customer's food order and a Coke refill, and she asked if there was anything else she could get her. Summer ordered a slice of apple pie with vanilla ice cream, but she told the waitress to bring it after she finished her food. Tess made the best apple pies, so Summer hoped the one from this diner would be good. After finishing her slice of warm apple pie, which was a close tie to Tess's, and getting her check, Summer left a $5 tip for the friendly waitress and proceeded to the cashier.

As she was paying her check, Summer asked the cashier, "Where's the nearest hotel?"

"There's a Best Western just down the road on the same side as the diner." "You can't miss it."

"Thanks," Summer replied.

"Where are you visiting from?" the cashier asked but Summer, who did not trust strangers, was not inclined to tell her. She retrieved the change from the cashier, thanked her, and walked out of the diner quickly and nervously. The fact that the cashier asked her where she was from along with the waitress Melinda staring at her intently made Summer very nervous, and she needed to get out of there. When she opened the door and heard the chime again, it rattled her even more, and she walked quickly, almost running to get into the safety of her car.

Outside, Summer looked back a couple of times to make sure she wasn't being followed. When she reached her car, she immediately got in. The thought of the waitress staring at her made Summer really uneasy, as if the waitress was able to read her thoughts and knew the reason why she was in Natchez. Inside the car, Summer anxiously made a call to Big Daddy.

"What are you doing in Natchez anyway?" Big Daddy barked. "I told you to lay low a day or two outside of town."

"I figured I could just get a hotel close to the entrance to town, and besides, I was hungry."

Trying to reassure her about their plan, Big Daddy told Summer, "Don't worry. No one knows who she you are or why you're there. You've been gone way too long for people to remember you."

7

Summer walked through the doors of the Best Western and stepped to the front desk. She immediately locked eyes with a vaguely familiar, yet unfamiliar face. Summer intently looked at the short, heavy set, dark-skinned lady with a naturally curly hairstyle. In return, the woman looked at Summer with a scouring look on her face. Summer turned around to look behind her and see if there was someone else the lady was looking at like that, but she was the only person in the lobby. The front desk clerk just stood there staring right through Summer with a scowl. Then, the lady, whose name tag read Char, opened her mouth, and with the nastiest attitude, spewed obscenities at Summer. Summer spewed her own obscenities right back. She was not going to let this chick talk to her like that. Somebody who didn't even know her, and especially since she was only trying to get a room.

Now you decide to show back up after we turn 21, huh?" she threw out.

"I don't even know you," Summer shot back.

"The heck you don't," the clerk yelled. "You've been gone since our 13th birthday, and now you decide to show up after ruining people's lives," Char continued. Upon hearing those words, Summer paused and stood frozen. With the gears turning in her mind, "Did she say 'our 13th birthday,'" Summer thought.

"Wait, who is this?" Summer thought to herself. "This can't be Charla," Summer whispered.

"Uh, yeah," Charla returned with attitude.

Summer began to break down in tears as she now knew the vaguely familiar face was her best friend Charla; a memory that she suppressed and locked away. Summer immediately turned on her heels and ran out the door of the hotel lobby to her car and jumped in. Sobbing uncontrollably, Summer barely heard the tapping on her car window. As the tapping continued, she looked up into the teary eyes of Charla. Summer motioned her to the passenger side of the car. Charla opened the door and slid her round, 5'2" frame into the tiny car. As soon as she closed the door, the two long lost best friends stared at each other and cried for what felt like an eternity. The two finally embraced. After they broke their embrace and dried their tears, Charla spoke first. She told Summer that she forgave her for leaving her all alone.

After Summer left, Charla immersed herself in church. After she received salvation at the age of 15, she learned how to forgive others and how to release things of the past. As a matter-of-fact, she had to quickly repent for some of the words that she spewed out of her mouth during her temporary moment of anger. Summer just sat quietly as her chest heaved up and down from the torrential crying she just finished. Charla told Summer to come back into the hotel so that she could check her into a room.

Summer got out of the car and grabbed her suitcase from the backseat where she'd thrown it in haste, and she followed behind Charla back into the Best Western. Charla checked Summer into a King bed room for 5 nights. After paying and retrieving her keys, Summer proceeded to the elevators to go to her room on the 3rd floor. Charla came from behind the desk and followed along. "There are a lot of questions that need to be answered," Charla responded to Summer's questioning hazel eyes. When they reached Summer's room where she'll be staying for the next 6 days, they both just sat on the bed in silence.

"Summer, what happened to you?" Charla asked with anger mixed with distress.

"I was being molested by Uncle Wil," Summer blurted out with a fresh new set of tears rolling down her cheeks.

"What?!" Charla yelled jumping from the bed. Summer repeated what she said and added, "My parents were on drugs, and they were using me as a way to get money to buy drugs."

Charla could not believe what she was hearing. There was no way on God's green earth that her Pastor, Pastor Wilburn Thibodeaux, was molesting her best friend as a child. Although Pastor Wil, as he's now affectionately known, wasn't a Pastor when they were kids, he's a Pastor now, and Charla and her family were faithful members of the church he pastored. Charla stood for a little while stunned at the words Summer just spoke, but when it finally hit her, she fainted onto the floor. When Charla came to, she got up and immediately rushed out of Summer's hotel room. She had to get away from her because there was no way that what Summer said was true.

Summer could not sleep that night. She was very troubled by Charla's reaction to her news, and now she worried that Charla didn't believe her. This angered Summer badly. Summer called Tess because she needed consoling. She asked Tess if she should just ax her plan and come back home. As Tess was telling Summer, "Yes, go ahead and come back home," Big Daddy snatched the phone away and went in on Summer. "Summer, I thought I told you to lay low for a couple of days. Why in the world did you go into that town already?" Big Daddy was upset and he was going to put an end to the nonsense talk. He told her that she was there on a mission, and he fully expected her to complete what she went there to do. When Summer hung up the phone, she was even more weary than when she first called. Summer just lay across the bed crying. She must have cried herself to sleep because she rolled over to her other side to avoid the sunlight that was hitting her face.

Summer rolled out of bed after she looked at the clock and saw that the time was 8:19 am. While grabbing her belongings to go take a shower, Summer's thoughts couldn't help but to wander to Charla. She thought about her old friend and how she rushed from the hotel room the night before, which brought on a fresh set of tears that flowed down her face. Her thoughts were quickly interrupted by the ringing of her cell phone. She reached down, grabbed it off the bed, looked at the screen, and saw that it was Kai. She answered the phone on the first ring because she was very surprised to hear from him since he hadn't called in a while. He was very cheerful on the other end, but Summer couldn't match his joy.

Sensing something was wrong because Summer wasn't usually as quiet with him on the phone, Kai asked, "Everything ok, baby girl?"

"I'm alright," Summer responded back.

"Naw, you lying, you ain't alright," Kai shot back quickly. "What's up?" In her mind, Summer wanted to tell Kai everything, but she knew she didn't have the nerves to do so. She didn't even tell him that she was leaving New Orleans.

"I'm on my way," Kai responded to Summer's silence.

"No, no. I'm not at home," Summer stammered out.

"What? That nigga got you out tricking this early in the morning," he spewed out with obscenities.

Since everyone in the local neighborhood knew each other, and everybody in town knew Big Daddy and his business, word had gotten out that Summer was also working for Big Daddy. This bothered Kai a bit when he first found out from some of his boys on the street, but when he confronted her about it, he just said, "Baby girl, I understand. Do what you gotta do to survive." And he left it at that. Even though Big Daddy tried to put an end to their relationship, she and Kai found ways to be together. But after a while, Kai stepped back from the relationship and said, "I don't want you to mix business with pleasure and get confused one day." This broke Summer's heart because she was hooked on Kai. Since he'd grown fond of her as well, he didn't cut off their friendship entirely, especially since he was like a protector to her.

"No, No," Summer stammered out again. "I had to go out of town for a few to handle some business but things aren't going so well," she told him.

"A'ight, I get it," Kai responded. "But I thought I was ya' boy, and you ain't even tell me nothing," he said angrily.

"I'm sorry," was all that Summer could say in a whisper.

"Bet," Kai responded and said, "Holla," before hanging up the phone.

This added a new set of tears to Summer's already red, puffy eyes. She hated to have disappointed Kai, but she just couldn't tell him the truth. They were so close, and surely she could have trusted him with her secret, but she couldn't muster up the courage to tell him.

Summer turned on the shower and let the water get as hot as she could stand it before getting in. Summer cleansed herself, and then she just let the water run over her face and down the front and back of her body as her tears mixed with the water. She didn't have to worry about her hair getting wet because her naturally curly, reddish-brown hair was the product of a bi-racial marriage between her white father and black mother. Summer never thought much of her looks because she suffered too much mental and physical trauma as a child, but she was constantly told that she was a beautiful ray of sunshine with her light-golden skin adorned with freckles on her dimpled cheeks that complimented her hazel-colored eyes.

Summer's low self-esteem never allowed her to accept the compliments others gave her, and when she looked at herself in the mirror, all she saw was a little girl whose innocence was stolen. But no one could tell that Summer dealt with low self-esteem, rejection, and abandonment. When she was with her customers, she acted as if she was a Goddess hidden behind light applications of makeup, fancy hairstyles, and designer clothes. She walked with her head held high and her shoulders square as if she had all the confidence in the world. But when she was home with the makeup off, her hair down, and the fancy clothes off, she let her shoulders slump and reveal how she really felt about herself. Feelings of guilt, shame, confusion, depression, and despair all plagued her thoughts day in and day out.

With her mind in la-la land, Summer slowly dressed in a mint green Lacoste T-shirt dress and white, strappy Prada sandals. Summer dressed really well. Even though she didn't feel as good as she often looked, she always dressed up to bring some kind of beauty to her dark, ugly inside. She pulled her hair up into a messy bun, put some lip gloss on her lips, pulled her Prada backpack over her shoulders onto her back, and headed out of her hotel room to go get some breakfast. All that crying throughout the night and morning made her famished.

Getting off the elevator, Summer immediately darted her eyes towards the front desk in anticipation of seeing Charla, but she locked eyes with a good looking, tall, chocolate young man instead. As Summer passed the desk, he gave her a sexy smile and uttered a bass filled, "Good morning. Did you have a pleasant evening?" Summer didn't know how to respond knowing that her evening was not pleasant at all, but in her soft spoken voice with down cast eyes, she responded, "I slept well," and quickly walked out of the door. When Summer reached her car, her hands shook as she tried to open the door. The guy at the counter made her nervous, but he also sparked something unfamiliar in her. Her face felt warm, and she felt a tingle in her thighs that she tried to ignore.

8

Summer pulled out of the hotel parking lot to head down to the *Eat in Route* diner. Pulling into the diner parking lot, she glanced into the car pulling out, and her heart began to pound as she saw Charla seated in the passenger seat. Charla's head was tilted slightly looking down as her lips moved, so she didn't even see her. Summer was thankful, disappointed, and nervous at the same time. She wondered if the driver was Charla's boyfriend, or even her husband, and if she was headed to work.

Entering the diner, Summer was greeted by the waitress Melinda from the day before, which made her nervousness intensify because of the woman's staring at her while she was leaving yesterday. However, Melinda gave her the warmest greeting and seated Summer in the same booth she was in previously. Summer ordered a cup of decaf coffee to start her morning. After the waitress returned with her coffee, she ordered scrambled eggs with cheese, crispy bacon, sausage links, and wheat toast with no butter. As she sipped her coffee and waited for her breakfast, Summer took several items from her backpack: a notebook, map, pen, books, and several other papers. She sprawled everything across the table so she could look over her plans and any other logistics she had to get in order.

By the time her food arrived, Summer was deeply engrossed in her plans, and she didn't immediately recognize that her waitress was standing there with her food. The "Excuse me sweetheart" she heard startled her, and she quickly closed her notebook and grabbed the books she had laid open in front of her. As the waitress placed her food before her, she asked if Summer was in school in which she replied with a sharp "No, I'm not." Melinda was truly taken aback by the tone of her response and uttered under her breath, "Lord, not today." Melinda, being the woman of God that she was, believed that every customer assigned to her tables was divinely directed. Last night, she talked with the Lord about the young lady she served earlier, and all she received from the Lord was the word "Love." She didn't expect she would need to walk in it specifically the very next day. "And how did I end up with her again?" Melinda thought to herself. Melinda was the sweetest, kindest, most loving woman anyone would ever meet, but this child was trying her love and patience early this morning.

"Enjoy your breakfast," Melinda forced out before she immediately turned and walked away. She did not wait for the unpleasant response she knew was on its the way. Melinda went to check on her other customers, and after seeing everyone was well, she went to her office. Melinda was the co-owner and manager of the *Eat in Route* diner, but she wanted to be hands-on with the customers and often performed the duties of hostess or waitress. She believed that her presence in this manner is what kept many of the local customers patronizing, and what also had customers passing thru singing the diner's praises, especially on review websites on the Internet. Melinda's son was a social media guru, so he managed the diner's social media sites and searched the Internet for reviews.

While in her office, Melinda began praying for God to show her what he wanted regarding the young lady seated in booth 8. She began to intercede in prayer for the young lady, and God revealed some alarming things to Melinda. She saw a lot of anger and rage in the spirit pertaining to the girl, and this troubled her spirit. She saw a gun, which troubled her even more, and she heard the word abuse. Melinda stayed in her office for about 20 minutes more, praying in the Holy Ghost, so that she could be directed on how to talk to and handle the young lady.

Melinda emerged from her office and went to check on her customers; she saved booth 8 for last. When she arrived at Summer's table to remove her empty dishes, Summer immediately snapped at her. "It's about time you came back. I needed a coffee refill and you were nowhere to be found. Good thing there are good employees around here to help the customers," Summer threw out. "I want to talk to the manager. Can you get the manager right now?" she barked out a little louder, not giving Melinda the opportunity to speak. "As you wish," Melinda threw out with a smile and turned on her heels. Other patrons within earshot looked on while Melinda smiled and nodded at them as she passed by.

After dropping the dishes into the kitchen, Melinda went back to her office. She removed her apron and hung it on the back of the office door. She walked over to her desk chair, removed the cardigan hanging on the back of the chair, and put it on. She adjusted her name tag, which read MELINDA in bold letters with General Manager underneath, and made sure it was straight on her cardigan. She walked over to her wall mirror and released her hair from its ponytail. Melinda grabbed her lipstick from her purse and touched up her lips. Leaving her office, Melinda walked back through the restaurant greeting and chitchatting with customers as she made her way back to the booth of the young lady who requested the manager. She approached the table, and before she opened her mouth to speak, the young lady looked up with a shocked look in her eye.

Melinda put on her best smile and said, "I understand you requested to speak with the manager." Summer sat and looked at Melinda with a fire in her eyes. This rattled Melinda.

"Oh, so you're the manager now? How are you the manager and a waitress?" Summer questioned.

"I am actually the general manager," Melinda replied pointing at her name tag. "I prefer to be hands-on with the customers. It makes for better business and customer service."

"Well, your customer service isn't good with me," Summer snapped. "You left me sitting here for a long time and I had a need," Summer told Melinda angrily with an attitude as her voice started to rise again.

Melinda slid into the empty chair across from Summer. As she settled in, she apologized to Summer for her extensive absence. She then asked Summer if she knew what being a Christian was. Annoyed by this question, Summer told her, "That's somebody who goes to church." That was not the answer Melinda was expecting, and she soon realized that this was going to be much harder than she thought. Melinda took her time responding because she wanted to be sure that she said the right thing, especially since the young lady was so upset.

"Have you ever heard of Jesus Christ?" she carefully asked.

"Yea!" Summer snapped sarcastically. "Get to the point lady," she continued.

With a smile, Melinda told her a Christian was more than someone who just went to church. "They believe in Jesus Christ and have given their life to live for him. I am a Christian." She explained to Summer that she was in her office praying to God, which delayed her return. Summer was annoyed and uninterested in what the lady was saying, while at the same time becoming fidgety in her seat.

Then she spat out, "So why are you sitting here? Don't you have some praying to do?" She told Melinda, "I'm out of here," and started grabbing her belongings.

Melinda spoke quickly and told Summer "I had actually been praying for you, and I hoped I would be able to sit and talk with you." Hearing this made Summer stop mid-course as she was placing her stuff back into her backpack.

"Talk about what?" Summer snapped. "Lady, you don't know me, and you don't have anything to talk to me about."

"You are correct," Melinda started. "I don't know you, but I would like to be able to talk to you about your anger."

"Look lady! I told you, you don't have anything to talk to me about," Summer shouted drawing the attention of the other diners.

Looking around, Melinda noticed everyone's attention was drawn to their booth, so she decided to call a peace truce. Sliding from the booth, she muttered, "Lord, now what?" and silently walked away. Melinda began interacting with the other diners, but her thoughts were perplexed. As she sat across from Summer, she was able to get a better and deeper look at her. She could have sworn that this girl had the strong features of a lady named Bernadette Wilks in her women's bible study group at the women's prison. "I have got to find out more about this child and if she is who I think she is," Melinda rambled in her mind.

9

After the confrontation with the waitress, manager, or whoever she was, Summer decided it was best to leave the diner and vowed never to return. She hurriedly packed her items into her backpack and quickly got up from the table to leave. Summer noticed the other customers staring at her as she walked up to the hostess station to ask for her check so she could pay it and leave. Melinda met her at the hostess station and said, "Breakfast is on me. Have a blessed day." Summer stood still for a few seconds, scowled at Melinda, then turned and walked away, rolling her eyes at the words, "Have a blessed day." When Summer got back into her car, she just sat there trembling for a very long time. Not moving or doing anything, she just stared straight ahead at the building of the *Eat in Route* diner. Then, her eyes fixed on the words, *"Jesus Christ is Lord,"* in the window of the diner. *"This is a church restaurant,"* Summer thought perplexed.

This visit to the diner unnerved and agitated Summer more than it did the first time she was there. She felt restless and needed to move about. She sped out of the diner's parking lot and quickly drove back to the hotel. Summer jumped out of her car and ran into the hotel. She moved swiftly past the front desk, daring not to look in that direction, and went straight to the elevator. After reaching her room, Summer paced back and forth in the moderate-sized room. Her thoughts were going a million miles a minute. There was a stirring in Summer when she was around Melinda that she couldn't quite explain. Flopping down on the bed, with her hands shaking, she pulled her cellphone from her bag to call Tess. She knew that Tess would know what to say and what to do. When Tess answered, Summer began to recant the happenings of her morning. Tess listened quietly. When Summer finally finished, Tess didn't have a response, or at least not one that Summer wanted to hear.

"Just calm yourself and don't worry about the woman," Tess responded lovingly. "Just focus on the reason why you are there." Summer went into a cursing fit, yelling at the top of her lungs. "You don't know what I'm going through and don't tell me to calm down." Tess was in shock because Summer had never disrespected her or talked to her in such a tone or attitude. Something had manifested in Summer. Tess decided to back down from the conversation. It was a good thing that Big Daddy wasn't around, otherwise, he would've dealt heavily with Summer and her attitude. Unable to calm down, Summer ended the call, jumped off the bed, and started pacing the floor again. She started to rethink her plan and thought it may be best to return home to New Orleans. She was really feeling unsettled in Natchez. Following her encounters with the

Melinda lady and with Charla, Summer was beginning to think she was crazy.

Melinda was not at all surprised that the young lady didn't say thank you before leaving after Melinda told her that her breakfast was on her. Melinda had to get some answers to the questions swirling around in her head these past two instances and to the discernment in her spirit regarding the mysterious girl. Melinda went into her office, removed her cardigan, hung it on the back of her office door, and plopped down into her desk chair. She reached into her pocketbook to retrieve her cellphone. She scrolled through her contacts until she landed on the number for Missionary Ruth Beam, who does prison ministry with her at the women's prison. When Sis. Ruth answered, she immediately started talking before Melinda could even greet her.

"Praise the Lord First Lady! You were just on my heart, and I was praying that whatever assignment the Lord has put into your spirit to do, that you would just obey even without full understanding." Melinda was a little taken back by what Sis. Ruth was saying, although, she shouldn't have been. Sis. Ruth was a true prayer warrior and a real intercessor, and she was always receiving a "right now, exact word" from the Lord. The things that Sis. Ruth had just spoken were what the Lord had placed in Melinda's spirit. Once Sis. Ruth finally took a breath, Melinda was able to get a word in.

"I was calling you about a woman we've visit with at the prison when we go. Her name is Bernadette."

"Yes, I know Bernie," Sis. Ruth interrupted. "Such a shame all that the child has gone through. She had such a bright future ahead of her and got mixed up with that no good Wilks boy that caused her to go down the wrong path. And look where she is now, in prison, got HIV, and done lost all her children; one ran away and others taken away by the state," Sis. Ruth rambled.

"That's what I was calling you about," Melinda cut in again when Sis. Ruth took a breath. "The one who ran away, about how old would she be right now?"

Thinking, Sis. Ruth was silent as she pondered, and then she answered, "She probably would be about 20 or 21 now. She left when she was 13. Nobody knows why that child done run away. Traumatized both Charlotte and her daughter Charla when they had to come back home from New Orleans that day without that child with them." Sis. Ruth talked on and on.

"Wait, did you say Charla?" Melinda asked cutting off Sis. Ruth. "You mean Charla from the church who works at the Best Western?" Melinda rushed out.

"Yes, that's where she works. Wait, what is going on?" Sis. Ruth asked finally catching on to what Melinda was asking. "Why are you asking these questions? Child, I got so caught up in talking and was not paying attention."

"It's ok Sis. Ruth," Melinda responded. "Well, Sis. Ruth," Melinda started, "I don't really know, but a young lady has come into the diner two days in a row now. And she appears to be from out of town, but she has an extremely strong resemblance to Bernadette at the prison."

"Lord have mercy," Sis. Ruth shouted. "Lord have mercy! I knew there was a reason my spirit was vexed, but I could not clearly discern it no matter how many times I done asked the Lord. This can't be good," Sis. Ruth cried out.

"Why do you say that Sis. Ruth?" Melinda asked.

"I don't know child, I don't know," Sis. Ruth responded in exasperation.

"Well, I must say that my spirit has been vexed as well," Melinda mentioned. "But I just thought it was light coming against darkness because the young lady has a very dark soul, and an extremely nasty attitude regardless of the amount of kindness that has been shown to her."

"This can't be good, Lord this can't be good," Sis. Ruth repeated to herself again. "Child, let me get off this phone and pray. I's got a whole lot of ground and people to cover. I'll see you at Prayer Meeting tonight First Lady," Sis. Ruth stated matter-of-factly in a rushed tone before hanging up the phone.

Everything Sis. Ruth said troubled Melinda all the more as she sat holding the cell phone in her hand. She began praying in the spirit, and she ended her prayer by asking the Lord for direction. Then, she remembered Sis. Ruth mentioned Charla. Melinda jumped up from her desk, grabbed her pocketbook and keys, and quickly left her office. She found her Asst. Manager Alex and told him that she'll be out for a few moments. She said bye to the hostess as she headed out of the diner. A little frazzled, Melinda headed towards her assigned parking spot and got into her brand-new Buick Regal, which was a birthday gift from her husband earlier in the year.

Melinda wasn't a very materialistic woman, but she thought the new car was a nice gesture since she'd been driving the same car for the past 12 years. Ever since she had married her highly successful and wealthy husband 5 years ago, he wanted to get her a new car, but she kept refusing. He didn't like that. Her husband felt like as one of the most prominent businessmen of the Natchez community and the Pastor of a growing ministry, his wife should have the best of everything. Melinda was a simple woman who didn't like to bring attention to herself because she desired that attention be brought to the Christ in her, instead.

Melinda drove the short distance to the Best Western hotel. She parked her car in the closest available parking spot she could find, turned off the ignition, got out, and proceeded to the entrance. When she entered, she walked up to the front desk where she greeted Charla with a smile, which was not immediately returned until a moment later when Charla forced a smile onto her face. Melinda was puzzled at this response from Charla because she was on the hospitality team at the church.

"Hello First Lady," Charla greeted Melinda with nervousness in her voice.

"Hey Sweetheart, how are you, your husband, and the kids?" Melinda inquired.

"We're all doing well," Charla responded as calmly as she could. "Is there anything I can help you with?"

"That's so good to hear," Melinda replied. "Actually, yes there is. I came here to ask you about someone."

Charla's heart began to beat more rapidly in her chest than it already was. Melinda continued, "There has been a young lady who has come into the diner twice now, and she has a strong resemblance to a woman we see in the women's prison during our visits. When I spoke to Sis. Ruth today, she stated that you were friends with the young lady when you were children. Do you know who I'm talking about?"

Charla's nervousness now became mixed with a fury that began to rise in her. Memories of her 13th birthday 8 years ago started to flood in. She thought about how it turned from a celebration to a tragedy. Charla and her mom spent hours upon hours with security and police searching for Summer in the amusement park and nearby areas. Several hours passed, and eventually, the police urged them to go home with promises to call as soon as they found Summer. The call never came. When Charla's mom would call the New Orleans Police Department, no one ever had any new information to provide, and it seemed as if they pretty much gave up on finding her. Charla cried for many years over the loss of her best friend, and now she just showed up out of the blue without warning after all these years later.

Charla quickly snapped out of her furious thoughts when Melinda called her name and asked her the question again. "Do you know who I'm talking about?"

"Yes ma'am," Charla responded softly, "She is actually a guest here in this hotel."

"Praise the Lord," Melinda responded with excitement. "You must be very excited to see your friend again," Melinda continued cheerfully. Charla didn't respond. "Can you tell me how long she's planning to be here?" Melinda asked after Charla failed to respond to her last statement.

"She's booked 'til the end of the week," Charla responded flatly, not matching Melinda's excitement about Summer at all.

"Good enough," Melinda stated. "Sis. Charla, will you be at the Prayer Meeting this evening? I would like to speak with you about this further," Melinda asked.

Just as Charla was about to let Melinda know that she would be unable to make it to Prayer Meeting tonight because her husband had to work, and she didn't want to bring her 2-year-old twin girls, the elevator dinged. Both ladies turned their heads in the direction of the elevators. When the doors opened, Summer emerged with her luggage in tow. With a puzzled look, Melinda turned toward Charla, who just shrugged her shoulders as if to say, "I don't know," then diverted her eyes back to Summer.

10

Following her phone call with Tess, Summer was angry and just ready to get out of Natchez again. She quickly threw her things back into her small suitcase and zipped it up. After looking around the room and glancing into the bathroom to make sure that she didn't forget anything, Summer left the room and entered the elevator preparing to leave the hotel. As she exited the elevator, she saw Melinda and Charla looking at her. Summer scowled internally and tried to walk pass them, but the lady from the diner stopped her.

"Excuse me sweetheart, I didn't get your name earlier" Melinda spoke politely.

"That's because I didn't give it to you," Summer gnarled rudely as she tried to walk on, but Melinda stepped in her way.

Melinda felt like this was her last chance to get the answer to the question she's been having for the past two days, so she went for it. "You have a very strong resemblance to a woman who is part of my bible study group at the women's prison. Her name is Bernadette,"

Melinda blurted out. She then held her breath hoping for a positive response.

Upon hearing her mother's name, Summer felt like she'd become paralyzed in her entire body; she couldn't blink, speak, or move. "Did this lady just say that my mother was in prison?" was the thought Summer was trying to process in her mind. Melinda could tell by the young lady's silence that she was on to something.

"Do you know who I'm talking about?" she inquired but still received no response. Summer continued to stand still in a state of mental, emotional, and physical paralysis. Charla decided to speak up.

"It's her mother. Ain't that right Summer?" Charla mocked nastily. When she heard those words, Summer's head turned in extremely slow motion toward Charla's voice as a lone tear rolled down her cheek. Summer's mind began to race as she thought, "This was not how this trip was planned." She was the one being confronted versus her confronting those who she came for. She clearly did not expect that she would run into people who knew her. She was supposed to come into town, find her abuser, unload the bullets from her gun into him, and then leave.

How did this happen? Summer seethed inside as she forcefully swiped at the tears now running down her cheeks. *"I am not weak. I will not be weakened,"* Summer repeated softly to herself over and over. That is what Big Daddy drilled into her for years: that she was not weak and that she would not show any signs of weakness no matter what.

"Summer, would you like to talk about it?" Melinda asked in a soothing tone.

"There is nothing to talk about," Summer said through clenched teeth. She tried once again to move on, but Melinda stood in her way. Melinda was looking down and reaching into her purse to get a business card out when Charla broke into the conversation.

With tears flowing down her face, "Well I think you need to talk about it! Talk about why you really ran away and why you've come back here to spread lies about innocent people," Charla spat out.

With fire in her eyes, Summer shot a piercing look Charla's way. She could not believe what she was hearing. Charla did not believe her when she told her that she was molested as a child. This infuriated Summer even more, and she forced her way around Melinda and blew through the door exiting the hotel lobby. When Summer walked out the door, Melinda turned to Charla with a slight wrath in her eyes for disrupting what she was trying to do.

"What was that all about?" Melinda asked Charla frustrated.

"She'll have to tell you herself," Charla responded with an attitude.

"Well, I guess that may not happen seeing as though she's gone now," Melinda shot back at Charla. Melinda turned to look towards the door, then looked back at Charla and said, "I must say that I'm slightly disappointed in you Sis. Charla."

"I'm sorry First Lady," Charla responded remorsefully. "But you have no idea the hell that Summer's leaving has caused and the hell her return will cause."

"Then maybe you should tell me about it," Melinda stated looking at Charla with scorning eyes.

"Sorry, no disrespect, but it is not my place or story to tell," Charla responded matter-of-factly.

Exasperated, Melinda turned to leave without saying another word. Melinda exited the hotel and headed straight to her car. When she got in, she leaned her head back against the headrest, closed her eyes, and cried out to God. "Lord, what is going on here and why does it feel like I'm losing control over a situation that I don't even fully have or know anything about?" Melinda lowered her head and ran her hand over her hair, which she forgot to put back into her signature ponytail. Suddenly, she caught movement out of her left peripheral. Slowly turning her head, she saw Summer in her car talking on the phone fast and making ferocious hand gestures and movements with her body. Melinda whispered, "Thank you Jesus," then she just sat still, careful not to run her off again. She sat in her car for a long 20 minutes waiting for Summer to end her phone call. When she heard the car start, Melinda quickly jumped out of her car to stop Summer from getting away again.

Melinda rushed around the car to the driver's side and tapped on the window. Summer looked in her direction with an annoyed and raging look like a lion ready to tear into its prey. "Why won't she go away?" Summer said out loud to herself very annoyed with this woman. She rolled her window down about one-fourth of the way. "Summer," Melinda started softly through the window crack, "I want to apologize for any offense I have caused you that has you so angry with me, but I would like the opportunity to start over." Summer just rolled her eyes. When Sumner didn't respond, Melinda continued, "You really piqued my interest and pricked my heart the first time you came into the diner, and I really would like an opportunity to talk with you, especially since I know your mother." Summer still didn't respond, even at the mentioning of her mother. She continued to stare straight ahead out of her front windshield as the tears began to well up in her eyes, which were hidden behind dark, large-framed Tom Ford sunglasses. The silence that continued from Summer told Melinda that she was at least thinking about what she was saying.

"I'll tell you what," Melinda started, "let me give you my card. Me and several ladies from the church get together on Tuesday nights for what we call a Chat & Chew prayer meeting. It's where women come together, share things they need help with, or just for prayer. Tonight we're meeting at a beautiful bakery called *Sweeties* just a few blocks down off the main road, and I would like to invite you to join us. You can just come, listen, and partake in the tasty treats that we'll have. You won't have to say anything, and I won't let anyone say anything to you. I promise." Summer still didn't move; she just sat motionless as she continued to stare straight ahead with her eyes fixed on a beautiful, pink blooming tree that was just across the parking lot.

"I'll be right back. I'm going to grab my purse from my car," Melinda said to Summer hesitantly before rushing over to her car to quickly grab her pocketbook. She pulled out a business card and a pen to write the address to *Sweeties* on the back. She tried to hand the card to Summer, but she still wouldn't move. Melinda slipped the business card in

73

the window seal hoping that Summer would roll down the window further to retrieve it. Turning on her heels, Melinda uttered, "I do hope to see you tonight, and if you don't want to come to the meeting, you can always call me and we can talk afterwards."

Melinda walked back to her car, got in, and started it up. On her car phone, she pushed the #3 speed dial button to call the diner to let them know that she would not be returning for the day. Melinda needed to go home and get before the Lord in prayer regarding the day's events as well as get clarity for the direction of the Chat & Chew prayer meeting tonight. She knew that Sis. Ruth was already praying. She always seemed to be two steps ahead of Melinda, but it was good to have such a strong prayer warrior on her team and in her corner.

When Melinda arrived home, she parked her car in the driveway instead of pulling into her usual spot in the 3-car garage of her and her husband's sprawling 4,000 square foot estate home. Her husband was out of town on business, so she knew he wouldn't need to get to the garage. Melinda's husband, who at the age of 38, was one of the most successful and prominent businessmen in the state of Mississippi, and he was an up-and-coming Pastor of a congregation of 400 members and growing for a church only 3 years old. Melinda was very proud of her husband's business success, but she was more elated at his success in ministry. Her husband was a very good teacher of the word of God. Melinda was raised by Pastors and had been a part of ministry all her life. Melinda would have only married a man who too had a major love and intimate relationship with the Lord and whose purpose was ministry.

Melinda met her husband at a small business association meeting in her hometown of Jackson when she was thinking of opening a restaurant. It was his continued references to God, the Lord Jesus, and the scriptures that he boldly spoke during his presentation that drew her attention to him. During the networking portion of the meeting, she was in a group that had been talking with Mr. Wilburn Thibodeaux. Melinda became even more smitten by him after he asked her to join him at his table for lunch, and the majority of the conversation around the table focused on biblical discussion. At the conclusion of the meeting, he made sure to search for Melinda to get her contact information before she left the conference center. From the very first call, they have been together ever since.

Melinda entered the house through the front door and went straight to her first floor office adjacent to her husband's. Closing the beautifully carved wood office door, she removed her shoes, got down on the floor, bowed her face to the ground, and began praying as fervently as she could about Summer and the topic for tonight's meeting.

11

Summer continued sitting in the car as she no longer knew what to do. She feared calling Big Daddy after Melinda left from inviting her to a prayer meeting. Summer didn't know much about prayer. Big Daddy would take her and Tess to church for Easter and Christmas every year, but other than that, there was never any talk about church or God. Her parents never took her to church. But Summer refused to believe in a God, who at Easter time the people in the church would say was love, who allowed the things that were done to her as a child. She was not going to a prayer meeting; there was nothing that could be done for her there. She will just have to advance with her plan sooner rather than later so that she could get out of town.

Summer wiped her tears, got herself together, and pulled out of the parking lot. She drove to a gas station she spotted a short distance away. She parked in a parking spot so she could think of a way to find out information on Wil's whereabouts. Summer got out of her car and went inside the convenience store to grab some snacks. Summer scoped out the young cashier she spotted after she walked into the store.

She figured she could grill him for the information she sought. She approached the cashier, placed her Coke, Doritos, and Hershey bar on the counter, and grabbed a pack of Orbit Sweet Mint gum. Summer pushed her sunglasses over her forehead to push back her unruly, curly hair from her face. As she did this, her hazel eyes were revealed, and as the male cashier looked up after ringing her items, he was immediately mesmerized by the beauty standing before him. Summer smiled knowing that her intention for going into the store was going to be accomplished. She engaged in small talk with the cashier whose name she learned was Barry. After paying for her items, she leaned on the counter chatting a little longer with Barry since there were no other customers. As she was leading the conversation to a close, Barry did exactly what she thought he would do and that was ask for her phone number. She pulled out her cell phone, snapped a quick selfie, and asked Barry for his phone number. After he gave it to her, Summer texted the seductive looking picture to him. Then, she asked for the information she sought; she asked Barry if he knew Wilburn Thibodeaux.

"Oh yeah, Rev. Wealthy Wilburn as I call him. Everybody in town knows him," Barry responded. "But I don't think he's in town. He travels a whole lot, but his wife owns the *Eat in Route* diner down the street," Barry volunteered.

Summer's stomach started turning at hearing those words, but a moment later, the corners of her mouth began to curl as a smile crept up to her lips. "Well, thank you Barry," Summer responded to this insightful information.

"You make sure you give me a call when you get off," she told him.

"I get off late," Barry said back to Summer.

"I'll be up," Summer threw back with a wink. She sashayed away from the counter as she exited the store knowing that Barry would be staring at the sway of her hips. Barry stood straight up thinking that today must be his lucky day to score the number of such a beauty on his first try.

Getting back into her car, Summer sat for a minute pondering the information that she'd just received. "Surely goodie-two-shoes, Christian, praying, talking to Jesus Melinda has absolutely no idea who she's married to," Summer thought to herself. "Well, she's about to find out," Summer said aloud. Happy with the thoughts that were going through her head, she reached into her bag and grabbed her Coke, opened the top, and took a big swallow of the cold, refreshing beverage. This did her well on this very warm 82° early spring day. She just sat in her car with a huge grin on her face at the thoughts running through her mind. Summer then looked to her left and saw the business card still secured in the sill of her driver's side window. She rolled the window down partially, retrieved the card, and looked at it front and back.

"Mrs. Melinda Thibodeaux, I think I just might join you at your little chat & chew meeting," Summer said to herself mockingly. "I have just the thing for us to chat and chew on," Summer said before breaking out in a rambunctious laughter. She was starting to feel a whole lot better despite the way things had started out. She didn't think it could get any better. The direction things were starting to go may be much better than her original plans for coming to Natchez. Her plan was to kill Wil, but if she could destroy his life and reputation instead knowing he would have to live the rest of his life in the aftermath, Summer would be A-OK with that too. "I need to call Tess," Summer thought to herself as she pulled her cellphone from her pocket.

Tess answered right away, "Hey baby girl. What's up?"

"I have some good news," Summer belted out excitedly.

"What is it?" Tess asked in anticipation.

"Well, after I got off the phone with you, I figured my plan would just have to be accelerated. I went to a gas station to get something to drink, and after talking to the cashier, I decided to ask about Wil, and he volunteered some valuable information." Summer said to Tess with so much cheer in her voice.

"I'm listening," Tess cut in.

"So, he tells me that 'Rev. Wealthy Wilburn' was not in town, but his wife was," Summer continued. "But guess who his wife is?"

"Who is that?" Tess asked inquisitively.

"The goodie, goodie lady who has been harassing me," Summer said sarcastically.

"Shut up," Tess cut her off, "You have to be kidding me."

"No, I am not and check this out. She just had the nerve to invite me to a chat and chew prayer meeting."

"What!" Tess screamed in laughter, "Oh my goodness, I don't even know what you're up to but this sounds good already baby girl."

Summer laughed with Tess and laid out her new plan. Tess let out a strong sigh of relief; she was so elated to hear this new plan of Summer's. Tess did not like the idea of Big Daddy sending Summer to Natchez to kill someone for revenge at all. Yes, what that man did to Summer was sick, disgusting, and wrong, but taking his life was not the answer. Tess and Big Daddy had many arguments over the days leading up to Summer's day of departure, but he just refused to listen to reasoning.

Summer's new plan was much better, although it would ruin people's lives, especially innocent people. Oh well! A child's life was ruined due to the selfishness of adults. Tess let Summer know that she was proud of her and of her decision to go with a less rage-filled plan of revenge. Before ending the call, Summer told Tess that she loved her and would call her tonight when she got back. Since she didn't officially check out of the hotel because she still had her room key, Summer bit the bullet and drove back to the Best Western. She grabbed her suitcase from the backseat and headed inside. When she entered, she looked at the front desk, but Charla wasn't there. So she figured she was cleared to go to her room. She arrived to the room, and put her key card in the door, and it opened right away. She went inside, put her suitcase on the bed, and opened it to find an outfit for the evening's festivities. Summer decided on a peach D&G jumpsuit with ruffled sleeves. As she looked at the jumpsuit, she wondered why she even packed it in the first place, but she figured it was appropriate for the occasion. She then pulled out a pair of nude, Gucci, jeweled flat sandals to adorn her feet.

Since she had an hour before the meeting was supposed to start, Summer laid across the bed for a little relaxation. She grabbed her phone and decided to send cute, flirtatious texts to Barry, the convenience store clerk she'd just met. She hadn't heard from Kai, so she decided to focus on Barry for the time being. Barry was excited to receive the texts from Summer and would sneak in responses in-between customers. As time winded down, Summer ended her texts and got up to get ready. Summer didn't want to arrive on time, as a matter-of-fact, she wanted to arrive quite late. She went into the bathroom to take a quick shower. After getting out, she pulled her hair back into a cute top bun and put on a light coat of foundation, a little bronzer, mascara, and her favorite Chanel lip gloss. She proceeded back into the room and took her time getting dressed and ready for a great evening of Chat & Chew.

After she was fully dressed, Summer gave herself a final once over, grabbed her Gucci cross body bag, and headed out. When she got into her car, she put the address in the car's navigation system, which said the location was 8 minutes away. She drove the short distance, and as she made the left turn as directed by the navigation, she saw the tall sign in front of her that read *Sweeties Bakery*. The town had changed so much that Summer hardly recognized it. She pulled up to the parking lot and saw there were quite a few cars there. This gave her a few butterflies.

After backing into a parking space and putting the car in park, she looked straight ahead, and saw a huge billboard that read "Wilburn & Associates, Innovative Services for Financial Success" along with a picture of Wil and two other people. Summer knew that face and smile anywhere; it was one that haunted her dreams many nights. Summer became paralyzed with fury after seeing this large picture of her abuser right in front of her, especially of him looking so happy. Seeing that billboard enraged Summer more and just added more fuel to the fire she was about to set. Acting on her thoughts, she reached down and pulled the gun from the compartment underneath her seat and looked at it. "I should just unload all these bullets right into that billboard," Summer yelled pointing the gun right at it. Summer sat for a few minutes longer contemplating what to do. Putting the gun back in its hiding place, she decided to continue with the plan that was currently in motion.

One hot Summer jumped out of her car and marched hard in the direction of the entrance to *Sweeties*. When she got to the door, she flung it open so hard it startled everyone causing them to look in the direction of the loud clank against the wall. The ladies had just concluded prayer a few minutes before, and Melinda stood to release the word that God had given her at home during her personal prayer time. With all eyes staring back at her, Summer stepped inside the quaint, light blue, contemporary style bakery and immediately began to feel uncomfortable. The same discomfort she felt the two times she encountered Melinda at the *Eat in Route* diner. But she pushed through the feeling and yelled, "You want to talk! Let's talk!" with a snide sneer on her face. Melinda didn't move, and no one said a word.

Summer stood in the open doorway for a long moment in their silence. She suddenly came to grips with herself as the discomfort returned and was ready to flee. But as she turned to walk back out the door, an elderly lady had grabbed her by the wrist and was trying to guide her into the building. "Come on in baby," the old lady said trying to pull Summer into the bakery, but Summer kept pulling to turn in the opposite direction. The older lady was persistent and continued pulling Summer in a loving manner. Summer slowly submitted to the gentle tones and touches of the elderly lady until she found herself standing in the midst of the bakery with ladies of various colors, sizes, races, and looks staring back at her with sweet, smiling expressions on their faces. Summer faintly heard welcome's coming from all over the space where the women were gathered.

"This was not how this was supposed to go." Summer mused inside, her brows furrowed from the frustration of another failed attempt at her plan of revenge. Unmoved by Summer's abrupt entrance and outburst, Melinda came over with a hearty smile to welcome Summer and urged her to have a seat, but Summer remained standing where she was. "You're in here now. Go ahead and have a seat," Melinda spoke softly. Summer moved in very slow motion to sit in the chair that had been placed behind her. It was like she was having an out-of-body experience. There was a strange stirring inside of her, like a war being fought. Next, a tall, heavyset, brown-skinned lady with a short, curly afro walked up to Summer and handed her a plate of appetizers

and treats with a cup of sweet tea. "I didn't know what you might like sugar, so I brought you a little bit of everything," the lady spoke in a cheerful husky voice. Summer uttered a, "thank you," that was barely above a whisper. She looked down at the plate filled with chicken wings, pinwheels, a sandwich halve, a mini quiche, fruit, a petit four, a mini cupcake, and a lemon cake slice. When Summer looked up from the plate, all of the women had turned their attention back to Melinda who was now standing back at the front of the café area of the bakery.

12

Melinda told everyone at the beginning of the meeting that she was expecting a guest. She told the ladies that the guest may be someone who may look recognizable or familiar to some, but she would greatly appreciate it if everyone would treat her as if they didn't know her. At first there were a few grumblings and objections, but Melinda firmly urged them to trust her and trust God with this delicate situation. During the chat & chew portion of the meeting, the guest hadn't shown yet, so everyone relaxed and went back to being themselves. After 7 o'clock had come and gone, Melinda looked towards the door ever so often in hope and expectation, but Summer hadn't arrived. When the clock showed 7:35, Melinda thought it was now time to move things further along. During her prayer time at home, God had given her a very eager message to share, and she was ready to give it so that the group could get to any discussions or prayer requests the ladies might have.

Just as Melinda stood in the center of the café and called the ladies to attention, a loud bang came from the entrance of the bakery. Everyone jumped and looked in the direction of the door, and there Summer stood as if she was coming in like a tornado. She yelled out, "You want to talk. Let's talk!" The Holy Spirit told Melinda to stand silent. As Melinda did not respond to the disruptive entrance and outburst, Summer just stood there for a long time as the ladies just stared back at her. Discerning that chaos was brewing, Sis. Ruth was first to move towards the entrance and the young lady standing in the doorway looking like a ball of fire. While Sis. Ruth moved toward the girl, Melinda whispered to the ladies that she was her guest. One by one, the demeanors' of the ladies began to soften, and they put on their welcoming smiles. After Summer finally took a seat, which took some loving cajoling from Sis. Ruth, Melinda moved back to the center of the café after welcoming Summer to the meeting.

"Ladies," Melinda started, "today, God placed a heavy burden on my heart that he wanted me to talk about and discuss in tonight's meeting. God wanted me to share with you ladies about getting over past hurts, pains, sins, mishaps, and unforgiveness and moving forward in love. One thing I know is that at some point in our life, we've all been hurt by someone or something."

"Amen" and "I know that's right" rang out from around the room amongst the group of 20 ladies in attendance.

"Some of us have experienced abuse from our family or others, whether it was physical, sexual, mental, or emotional abuse." As Melinda spoke, a new fury began to stir in Summer knowing that she was abused by the very man Melinda was married to. She wanted to speak out, but instead she stayed silent. Melinda continued, "Some have experienced rape, abandonment, rejection, molestation, tragedy, or trauma. Yes, these things happened. Some of us were hurt more badly than others because of what we experienced or went through in our life." The room was eerily silent as the women listened intently thinking about their own personal lives. "Let me share with you a story about myself."

"My sophomore year in high school I did something that I should not have done. As you all know, I was the child of Pastors, so I've always been raised up in the church. Well, there was a guy at my high school who I was smitten with, and he liked me as well. He was on the football team; he wasn't one of the popular players, but when the others found out he liked me, they started to influence his interactions with me. I was considered one of the pretty girls in school, and several of the most popular athletes tried to get with me, but I wouldn't budge. I didn't want to become another notch on any of their belts. One Friday, he invited me to a party that one of the senior cheerleaders was having. I knew that my parents wouldn't willingly allow me to go, and I really wanted to go and spend time with him. That night, I begged my parents to let me go spend the night at a classmate's house whom I really didn't have a relationship with, but I knew she was going to the party. They reluctantly agreed, and I couldn't have been more elated."

"I arrived at her house, and shortly afterwards, we left for the party. The guy was already there when we arrived, and he and I immediately became engrossed in one another. I noticed he smelt like he had been drinking, but I didn't say anything at first. As I witnessed him drinking more and more as the night went on, I asked him to stop, but he ignored my requests. Instead of getting away from him or leaving, I dealt with it. During the night, we danced a little, talked, and hung with others until he wanted to be alone with me. Nervously, I agreed, and we went into the house. We sat on the couch and talked some more, then the talking turned to kissing, the kissing turned to touching, and that was when I stopped him. I told him that sex was not something I wanted to engage in with him at that time. He backed off, and we just started kissing again. Then he started touching me again, but that time a little rougher. I jumped up from the couch and tried to get away from him, but he pulled me back down." Melinda paused for a moment to take a deep breath before continuing her story. She noticed that every woman was either sitting straight up or on the edge of their seat listening intently, including Summer.

"He started to talk very bad to me, calling me a tease and cursing me out. Those words stung coming from him. He was such a sweet, humble guy. We were on the couch tussling as I continued to try to get away, and he was trying to keep me from doing so. Then several other guys and girls walked in and saw what was going on, but instead of breaking it up, they were encouraging him."

"Long story short, that night I left the house party battered, beaten, and raped by multiple guys. Afterwards, I was tossed out as if I came to the party uninvited. Even the girl who I went to the party with didn't even come to my rescue; no one did. I had walked about 5 miles not knowing where I was going before I ran into someone who saw my distress and drove me to the hospital. The police were called while I was in the emergency room, and they were dispatched to the house and arrested everyone at the party. I begged the hospital not to call my parents, but my parents had to be present due to the condition that I was in as a minor, which required me to stay overnight due to a beaten face, a broken wrist, 3 cracked ribs, and the performing of a rape kit. I couldn't tell them what actually happened, so I lied. I told them that me and the girl whose house I was at were out at the park and some other girls jumped us, but she ran away and left me when I couldn't get away. Needless to say, a month later, I found out that I was pregnant and my son was the product of rape. A judge ordered DNA tests from every male arrested at the party to determine paternity of my son, which turned out not to be the guy I liked."

"It wasn't until I graduated college, which was barely, before I finally told my parents the truth. I could no longer live with the pain and suffering of the trauma I experienced. I needed healing in a bad way; I needed to be free from the bondage of unforgiveness towards those who had done wrong to me." Melinda paused once again, this time taking a sip of her drink. She noticed that some ladies had tears running down their faces, but she also saw a very pained and strained look on Summer's face. She discerned that something she'd said was possibly reaching her. Continuing, Melinda told the ladies, "I didn't want to hurt anymore, and I needed to forgive and release every person that played a part in my traumatizing experience that night. I had been receiving counseling while in college, but I needed a spiritual healing. My parents were devastated when I told them, even though so much time had passed. My parents sent me away to their spiritual parents and mentors' church in Houston, TX so I could receive counseling and healing, which was an awesome and refreshing experience. I spent a year there, and I became free. I forgave those who hurt me, and now I'm living a great life."

"Today, God laid it upon my heart to share my story with you ladies. I haven't shared my story with many people, but God told me that my testimony is the help other ladies need to be free from their past and to be free from hurt, pain, rejection, abandonment, tragedy, and trauma. I know and understand that people may have hurt you. But you are hurting yourself more by holding onto the pain and anger. The other persons have gone on with their lives, and you're still living your life in those moments that happened to you at age 10, 13, 16, 21, or whenever years old." Summer was taking in everything Melinda was saying and actually pretty stunned at the things she was hearing. When Melinda started saying the ages, she lifted her head and locked eyes with Melinda. Summer shifted her gaze as tears started to well up in her eyes.

"I sense by the spirit of God that what I have said has stirred some of you. I want you to be free, I want you to be healed and whole, and I want you to live a life of happiness and peace. I want to just love on you and pray for you, so I invite you to come up." Melinda appealed to the ladies. "If you have suffered from anything I mentioned this evening: abuse, hurt, rejection, trauma, abandonment, or death, I invite you to come and let me pray for you." Several ladies began to move and go up to Melinda. Although Summer felt like she was the only one in the room and Melinda was talking directly to her, she refused to go up. Summer rose from her chair, leaned down to put the plate of uneaten food in the chair, and turned to head out the door. As she was trying to walk away, the same old lady was right there gently nudging her in Melinda's direction. *"Who is this old lady?"* Summer thought to herself annoyed.

"No, no. I'm leaving," Summer whispered with her voice quivering as she tried to choke back tears.

"It's ok baby, you don't have to leave. God can and will heal you from the hurt you're in." Sis. Ruth pleasantly replied to Summer.

"Excuse me," Summer said as she tried to go around Sis. Ruth, "You don't know what you're talking about."

"Oh, I do baby," Sis. Ruth whispered sweetly, "But it's not my place to say, but to pray."

Summer just stood there staring at the old lady like she was crazy. In-between praying for the other ladies, Melinda observed the exchange between Sis. Ruth and Summer, and she hoped that Summer didn't get away. As Melinda ended her prayer with the last lady before her, Sis. Ruth pointed towards Melinda and lovingly said, "Your turn." Sis. Ruth then prodded Summer a little more, but by that time, Melinda had moved closer to where they were standing. As Summer turned towards the gesture to Melinda, Melinda lightly grabbed her in a loving embrace. She held onto Summer gently at first not saying anything, and as she did so, Summer broke down crying.

As Summer cried, Melinda whispered the words of the Holy Ghost. "It's ok, you're safe. No one is going to hurt you or touch you anymore. I am so sorry for what your parents did to you, and what those men did to you. And I hate that you had to run away and what you're enduring now." Melinda started to pray, "Father God, I thank you for your daughter, this precious gem. I pray for her to be free from the hurt she's endured and had to live with for all these years. I pray for deliverance for her right now to be free from trauma, rejection, and abandonment. I curse every perverse spirit that has attached itself to her in Jesus' name, and I speak healing and say to you daughter be free. Release the hurt, release the pain, release the people, forgive, and let it go in Jesus' name." Summer cried even harder. Melinda continued to embrace Summer even more. As she did, Summer felt like she was being held in strong arms and that everything she had gone through was leaving her body at that very moment. She felt the love she didn't get from her mother, and she felt the protection she didn't get from her father. She felt a genuine wanting of her and not just people wanting her for what she could do for them.

Summer stayed in Melinda's embrace for what seemed like eternity. She felt safe and comforted. After Summer's cries steadied, Melinda spoke to her about salvation. When Summer acknowledged that she understood what Melinda was saying, she said, "I need you to repeat after me. God, I know that without you I am lost. The bible says that if I confess with my mouth and believe in my heart that Jesus was raised from the dead, I will be saved. I repent of my sins committed in my body. I confess

Jesus Christ as Lord. Amen." Melinda, Sis. Ruth, and two other ladies who were hanging around cheered at Summer giving her life to Christ.

Melinda was excited that God's purpose and plan for tonight's meeting was accomplished. Melinda learned over the years that if she yields to exactly what God has willed then everything will turn out just right. After Summer gathered herself, Melinda thanked her again for coming and welcomed her to the body of Christ. Sis. Ruth embraced Summer and said some encouraging words. The ladies then gathered their belongings so that Dianna, the owner of *Sweeties,* could lock up. The ladies walked out of the bakery together and walked Summer to her car.

When she got in, Summer just sat for a few moments pondering what all just happened to her. She also sat there refusing to look up at the billboard across the street that she knew was staring back at her. Summer started the car and quickly drove out of the parking lot. Her cell phone buzzed, which indicated she had a message. At the light, she pulled it out to check. It was Barry telling her he was getting off in 20 minutes and wanted to see her. Summer pulled off when the light turned green and drove the short distance to the Shell gas station. She went inside, although she knew she was a disheveled mess. Barry perked up when he saw Summer enter the store, but he then became alarmed because, although she was looking cute, her face looked a distressed mess far from the cute, freckled baby face he'd seen earlier. Summer explained to him that an emergency had come up, and she had to get back home. She promised to keep in touch. Barry was very disappointed at what he was hearing, but he told her that he understood. So this wasn't his lucky day after all like he initially thought it was when he'd gotten Summer's number earlier.

Summer quickly left the store, got back into her car, and sped the even shorter distance to the hotel. She jumped out of the car and swiftly walked into the hotel. She was glad to see no one at the front desk, so she was able to go straight to the elevator undisturbed. When the elevator doors opened, a young couple was on, so she stepped to the side so they could get off before she got on. When the elevator doors opened on her floor, she dashed off and walked fast to her room, which was three quarters of the way down the hall. Inside, Summer quickly began gathering her things from the bathroom and bedroom and tossed them into her suitcase. She closed the suitcase then gave the room a quick scan, and when she saw that nothing was left, she left the room as quickly as she came and headed back to the elevators.

Reaching the lobby, she made her way over to the front desk clerk to check out. It was the handsome guy she saw previously, but Summer sighed hoping he would not try to flirt with her. Because she had to keep it moving, she hurriedly told him she was checking out. Anthony, his name tag read, tried to make personal small talk, but when she wouldn't bite, he moved on to processing her check out.

"Your room is booked for another 4 nights," Anthony informed Summer.

"Yes, I know, but I have to leave for an emergency," she responded flatly.

"Yes, I understand. I must let you know that since you are cancelling the additional nights with less than a 24 hour notice, you will be charged for the next night, and I can credit you the other three nights," Anthony explained.

"Fine," Summer shot back disgruntled. "Just hurry up please."

With the checkout process complete, Summer darted out the door to her car, opened the trunk, and tossed her suitcase inside before getting into the car. Summer pulled out of the hotel's parking lot preparing to leave Natchez once again. As she was drove pass the *Eat in Route* diner, she cut her eyes over there wondering about what happened to her in that place during her first visit as well as tonight. After she passed the diner, Summer hurriedly drove the next 3 miles to get on the interstate to head back to New Orleans. Although she was in a rush and eager to get back, she knew she had to maintain a certain speed limit on the highway. She didn't even call Tess or Big Daddy to let them know that she was coming; she was just going home.

13

During the 3-hour drive, all Summer could think about was all the events that transpired over the past two days she was in Natchez and how not one thing went according to her plan. Now, she was returning to New Orleans, but as a different, yet strange person. The burdens she felt were no longer there. The anguish and anxiety weren't there either. She felt lighter and freer. Summer didn't know exactly what it meant to be saved, but she knew there was something different about her; she didn't feel any anger or hurt, there were no bad thoughts plaguing her mind, and there were no negative emotions that consumed her the way they had over the years. She felt herself smiling like she was no longer ashamed or empty. Summer pulled down the sun visor and looked in the mirror; she still looked the same, but she felt totally different.

Summer entered New Orleans and continued to drive the 25 minutes to where they lived in Gentilly. She really wanted to give Kai a call and let him know that she was back, but she quickly dismissed that thought. She pulled her car in front of the house and jumped out leaving her suitcase in the trunk. It was 2:30 am. She did not want to cause a stir going into the house unexpected, so she thought she'd better call before going in. Big Daddy was trigger happy and would shoot first and ask questions later. So, she slowly returned the screen door back to its closed position and pulled her cellphone from her purse. She called Tess's phone. Startled, Tess answered on the third ring. Summer told her, "I'm outside. Come to the door." Thinking the worse had happened with Summer back so soon and at such a late hour, Tess jumped up out of bed and rushed to the front door.

"Baby, what's wrong, what happened?" an alarmed Tess asked nervously as she opened the door and wrapped Summer in her arms.

"I'll tell you all about it in the morning," Summer said tired and groggily from the late night drive. "I just really need some rest," she told Tess.

"Ok sweetheart, we'll talk in the morning. Get some rest." Tess released Summer from her embrace. Summer stumbled to her room, opened the door, and fumbled her way to the bed. She just threw herself across it without even shedding the clothes she was wearing.

Late the next morning, Summer was abruptly awakened by Big Daddy storming through her room and standing over her. He wanted to go in the room at 2:30 am when Tess told him that Summer had come back, but Tess stopped him. Summer said a sleepy, "Good morning," barely above a whisper and tried to lift her head, but it was really heavy from the tiredness. Big Daddy didn't care if she looked like she needed more rest; he said, "We need to talk."

He was very upset with Summer because he hadn't heard from her since she'd left town. Then she just returns earlier than she was supposed to and unexpectedly in the middle of the night. "Ok, let me wash up," Summer spoke in a whisper. Big Daddy turned and walked out of the room, slamming the door. Tess was in the kitchen nervous about the confrontation that was about to take place. She exhaled the breath she'd been holding when she heard Big Daddy enter the living room and plop down on the leather sofa.

Summer rolled out of bed, stretched, and let out a long, lengthy yawn. Walking over to her dresser, she stared at herself in the mirror for a moment. She shook her head at the disbelief of how her life had unfolded over the past couple of days. The years of stuff within her was just gone in an instant. She opened the dresser drawer and took out fresh undergarments and something to lounge in so she could go take a shower. Several minutes later, Summer finally emerged from her room and trotted across the hall to the bathroom. She turned on the shower to warm the water then brushed her teeth. She stepped out of last night's outfit and got into the shower. Summer let the water run over her body, but when she tossed her head back under the shower head, the water running down her face mixed with tears as her mind began to process what happened to her last night. Her cry got a little stronger, harder, and then louder until she was wailing like a baby who was crying out for a bottle. Summer became overtaken by the encounter she experienced spiritually and emotionally. Eventually, her cries calmed, and she begin to cleanse her body just as her soul was being cleansed through her tears. Summer turned off the shower, stepped out, wrapped her towel around her body, and stood staring at herself in the foggy bathroom mirror.

"*What happened to you?*" Summer questioned her image. "*What did you do? How did you let something like that happen? You left to get revenge on someone else and ended up getting saved. What does being saved even mean?*" Summer ran off the questions to herself in the mirror. She didn't even know anyone who was "saved." Summer continued to stand in the small bathroom, not moving, speaking, or thinking. She was just in a daze not knowing what she was going to do from that moment forward. She dressed, walked back to her room, and sat down on the bed. She just sat there. Her cell phone dinged. She reached over to grab it from the nightstand and saw that she had several text messages from Barry trying to check on her. She replied, "Thanks," told him that she was well and had made it to her destination, and that she had been resting awhile. The two texted each other back and forth for a few moments until Barry had to return to helping his customers. Summer really wanted to call Kai. He was very wise and could probably give her some insight into her experience. But her pride wouldn't let her make the first call.

Summer tapped on the Google app on her phone and searched, "What does it mean to be saved." She clicked on one link and began reading. As she read, she found that being saved meant to turn away from a life without God. "To get saved means you decided to give up your selfish desires, needs, wants, pleasures, comforts, and egos. It means to give up power and control over your own life. You

99

get saved from a life of destructive behaviors that destroy you rather than build you up, such as alcohol, drugs, sex, abuse, the pursuit of money, and evil acts."

The webpage went on to say, "Involvement in those kinds of activities, habits, or behaviors come from the need to fill a void missing from your life or to fulfill inadequacies. When you get saved, you let God become a part of your life, and he fills that void. Getting saved causes you to reevaluate your life, how you're living, and what you're doing so you can make improvements. It's kind of like a wake-up call by God so that you can have a chance to make changes to how you're living morally before something tragic happens, like death."

After reading from the website, Summer sat in silence with her thoughts. She knew that she had destructive behavior; she was a prostitute for goodness sake. She cursed, drank alcohol regularly when she worked, and occasionally smoked cigarettes and weed. Summer began to ponder the damage that she was doing to her life, body, and even her future with her present lifestyle and behaviors. But it wasn't entirely her fault that she was this way. She was forced into this at 10 years old when her parents exchanged her for drugs. "What kind of positive future could I have as a prostitute?" Summer questioned herself. "Heck, Tess has been one for the past 16 years. Is that how the rest of my life is supposed to be lived out?" Summer thought intently. Tears once again began to roll down her cheeks as she sat thinking about her past, present, and future, which wasn't looking so promising. She was going to have to make some decisions, and some were going to be harder than others to make.

As Summer sat there, she heard movement in the front of the house. She wiped her face, arose from the bed, and walked to the living room where she saw Big Daddy and Tess entering. They must have left the house while she was in the shower. When they locked eyes, Big Daddy had a scowl on his face as if he was about to devour Summer the way a lion devours its caught prey. This made Summer really nervous, especially since she was going to have to tell him that the plan they worked so hard to construct had been blocked and by God apparently.

"I'm listening," Big Daddy belted out while staring deep through Summer's soul.

Summer begin to tremble nervously. "Summer, girl you better get to talking and you better do it fast!" Big Daddy boomed, his voice a level higher while he walked towards Summer.

"I...I...I didn't do it," Summer stammered out with her voice quivering as she stayed put in her spot.

"So what did you do then girl since you are back here and not one phone call from you?" Big Daddy yelled taking another step closer to Summer.

"I um...I um," she stuttered and stopped as she looked into his piercing gaze. Lowering her head and her voice even lower, Summer said, "I got saved." She closed her eyes and winced, bracing herself for the blow that she knew was coming next.

"You did what?" Big Daddy responded loudly. His 6'4" frame was standing now toe to toe with Summer.

Lifting her head and looking him straight in his piercing root beer-colored brown eyes, Summer repeated the three words, "I got saved."

Big Daddy grabbed Summer by her neck, but Tess immediately jumped in begging him to release his hold. He released her and stood there looking down on her with a face hard as stone. Big Daddy stared Summer down for a very long time before he turned to walk out the door, yelling behind him for Tess to follow. Tess looked at Summer with a smile on her face, happy tears welling up in her eyes, and mouthed, "I love you," before turning to follow Big Daddy. Right where she stood, Summer dropped to her knees and did something she never did before in her life: she prayed. "God, Jesus, I don't know if you hear me, but I need you. Amen," she whispered. She bowed her head and cried tears of relief the same way she did the night she got saved. Summer was still in the same position hours later when Big Daddy returned with Tess on his heels pleading with him.

"Summer, get dressed so you can get to work," Big Daddy commanded. Summer raised her head and lifted her hazel eyes up to him with a pleading look.

"I said get up girl and get dressed!" Big Daddy yelled down to Summer.

Summer slowly raised herself up with a fresh set of tears welling up in her eyes. "I can't do it anymore," she said.

"Oh yes you can and you will," Big Daddy belted out. "I don't know what they did to you down there in Natchez, but I'm running a business here, and you got to earn your keep little girl," he continued. "Now I said go get dressed for work," Big Daddy said a little louder and firmer.

Through her tears, Summer continued to plead with Big Daddy. "Please don't make me go! I can't do it anymore! I'm not going to do it anymore!" she said boldly.

Big Daddy reached down and grabbing a hand full of Summer's hair, he pulled her up to standing and threw her into the couch. "Don't you tell me what you not going to do. I own you girl," he yelled. He then went over to her and started landing punches into her body. Summer yelled out in pain with each blow from his fists. Tess, who could no longer watch, jumped on Big Daddy to pull him away from Summer and yelled for Summer to run. Summer took the out and darted out the door, wincing in pain with every step she took. Big Daddy slung Tess off him and went after Summer. By the time he got out the door, she had gotten out of the yard and down the street. Big Daddy went back into to house and began to stomp Tess where she lay. Big Daddy did not tolerate his girls getting out of line with him. He didn't like to beat them because the essence of his business was the fact that he had top-notch, beautiful, unbruised, and unbattered women. But these two pushed him over the edge today.

Outside, Summer ran down the street until she reached Mrs. Robertson's house, the lady who tutored her for years. She knocked on the door in a panic and out of breath. When Mrs. Robertson opened the door, she looked through the screen and saw Summer standing there with a look of distress. "What's wrong baby," she asked. Mrs. Robertson had grown very fond of Summer while tutoring her, and Summer still visited her at least once a week even though her tutoring was over years ago. "Mrs. Robertson, may I please come in?" Summer asked out of breath. Mrs. Robertson unlocked the screen, pushed the door open, and stepped to the side so Summer could enter. She looked outside to see if anyone was out there, and when she saw nothing or no one, she secured the screen lock then closed and locked the front door.

Mrs. Robertson asked Summer what happened, and she rambled off what took place down at the house following her admitting to Big Daddy that she had gotten saved. There was a glimmer in the old lady's eyes as she listened to Summer's announcement. Although Mrs. Robertson went to the same church she's been going to for the past 52 years, she didn't really like to talk to people about religion. She didn't like to step on people's toes, and she felt that if they wanted to live how they were living, then "let 'em be." So when Summer was coming to her for tutoring from the pimp's house, she never said anything. She just did the job she was paid to do, which was tutor the girl and graduate her with a home-school diploma. Mrs. Robertson was one to mind her own business. She never even asked questions about where the child came from, and the girl never talked about it either. As a matter-of-fact, she barely talked at all. The girl was very bright and smart, and she enjoyed their tutoring sessions because learning for Summer came easy; a trait that Summer knew she inherited from her mother.

Summer asked Mrs. Robertson if she wouldn't mind if she stayed there for a while until she could figure out what she would do. Mrs. Robertson was delighted to say yes and to have some company in the house. She wasn't tutoring any children at the time, so she was a little lonely. Summer used Mrs. Robertson home phone to call Tess since she left her phone at the house, but Tess didn't answer. She left a voice message letting her know where she was and to give her a call when the coast was clear. Little did Summer know, Tess was taking the beating that was meant for her.

Summer waited and listened to Mrs. Robertson as she talked on and on. Then, Mrs. Robertson arose and said, "I'm going to go fix us something to eat." "The girl is so skinny she needs a good meal," Alberta Robertson mumbled to herself. While in the kitchen preparing a meal of baked chicken, broccoli casserole, green beans, and rolls, Mrs. Robertson continued to talk to Summer, who was barely listening. When dinner was done, the two sat in the dining room and ate the prepared meal. Summer was a little worried as she bit into the food; she didn't know what to expect considering the old-fashioned decorated, moth ball smelling home. During her tutoring sessions, Summer only received snacks from Mrs. Robertson that included chips, cookies, crackers, sometimes sandwiches, and drinks.

However, Summer was pleasantly surprised by the meal. The chicken was tender, juicy, and seasoned very well. The broccoli casserole was cheesy and delicious. The green beans were just as good, and the buttery homemade rolls melted in her mouth. The food was so delicious that there was not a morsel left on Summer's plate, and as she asked Mrs. Robertson for seconds, a faint smile spread across the old lady's face. She hadn't had anyone to cook for since her husband passed away. Her children lived out-of-state now and rarely came to visit.

It felt good to know that she could still bless the soul through the stomach with her top chef cooking. Her family always liked to gather at her house for her meals, but after her late husband died, the family seemed to have died with him. While Summer sat and ate the second plate of food put before her, she was bemused that Tess hadn't called her back by now, seeing as several hours had passed. Summer called again, and Tess answered, "Hello," barely above a whisper. Her mouth was swollen from the blows she received. Tess winced as she as she tried to talk. Alarmed and sensing something was not right with Tess, Summer asked what was going on.

"He beat me up," Tess cried.

"Oh no, I'm coming back down there," Summer cried herself.

"No, don't," Tess begged. "I'll be ok. I'll take care of myself." But Summer wasn't hearing it.

She hung up the phone and told Mrs. Robertson that she had to go check on Tess, and she would be right back. Summer dashed out of the house and ran back down the block to their house. As she neared, she stopped dead in her tracks at the sight that was before her eyes. Summer walked slowly toward the yard with her hands covering her mouth. She saw that every window had been broken out of her car, and all four tires were flattened. Summer became even more devastated at the sight of all of her clothes, shoes, handbags, and just about everything from her room, minus the furniture, all strewn over the front lawn. Summer could not believe that Big Daddy had gone this far in his anger. He cared more about himself and his business than her life.

Summer sobered up real quick from seeing her belongings everywhere and remembered why she was there in the first place, Tess. Since Big Daddy's car wasn't in the driveway, she rushed into the house. She called out to Tess as she went from room to room looking for her. She finally found her lying on the bathroom floor beaten, battered, and bloody. Summer had never seen such a sight, and she cried out for her friend and mother figure. It had been a very long time, years even, since Big Daddy had laid a hand on either of them. Summer felt terrible that Tess had taken such a beating on her behalf. She cried, "I'm sorry, I'm so sorry," over and over again. She kneeled down and pulled Tess into a gentle embrace, and they cried together.

Tess urged Summer to go and get out the house before Big Daddy returned. Tess begged Summer not to call again, and she promised to call her in a couple of days. Summer didn't want to leave Tess in such a state, but she also didn't want the same thing to happen to her. So, she slowly got up and reluctantly left Tess. Before leaving, she stopped by the kitchen and grabbed some trash bags. Summer then made her way out of the house to gather her belongings off the lawn. She gathered up her clothes, shoes, underwear, jewelry, pictures, and handbags and hurriedly tossed them in the trash bags.

After gathering up the last of her things, Summer struggled as she dragged the four trash bags filled to capacity down the street to Mrs. Robertson's house. She was exhausted by the time she finally reached the house. Mrs.

Robertson was sitting on the porch awaiting her return. When she saw the trash bags, she quickly arose alarmed.

"What's all that baby?" she asked.

"Mrs. Robertson, Big Daddy threw out all my stuff," Summer told her.

"It's ok sweetheart. I got room." Mrs. Robertson pulled open the door to let Summer bring her belongings into the house.

After settling into the bedroom she would be staying in, Summer dumped all the bags on the floor in an effort to find her cell phone, which she didn't exactly recall picking up. Thinking about all that Big Daddy had done to her other stuff and the car, there was no telling what he did with the phone. Summer trotted to the telephone and dialed her number. She listened for her phone to ring, but she didn't hear any ringing in the house. She laid the cordless handset back in its cradle. Exhausted from the day, Summer decided it was best to go to bed. She said good night to Mrs. Robertson and retreated to the room. She got in bed and allowed herself to fall fast asleep.

The next morning, Summer awoke to the smells of Mrs. Robertson cooking breakfast. Although awake, she didn't get out of bed right away. Summer just laid there thinking not only of the events that happened last night, but also about everything that happened over the course of the week. She really wished that she could just talk to Tess, but she had to wait for Tess to call her. After about an hour of lying there thinking, Summer got out of bed and walked across the hall to the bathroom to wash up.

After she emerged from the bathroom, she went to the kitchen looking for Mrs. Robertson, but didn't see her. She found her instead in the living room sleeping in a recliner with a newspaper in her lap. Not wanting to wake her, Summer went back to the kitchen. On the stove, she saw a covered plate, that she assumed was for her. She removed the aluminum foil to reveal light, fluffy eggs, bacon, sausage links, hash browns, and biscuits. Everything smelled so delicious, and she couldn't wait to dig in. She put the plate in the microwave for only 10 seconds so as to not disturb the food's original cooked state. Summer sat at the table and devoured the best home-cooked breakfast she'd ever had.

Tess was a really good cook, but there was something rich and special about Mrs. Robertson's cooking. "If I keep eating like this, I'm going to put on a few pounds," Summer mumbled in between bites. "Oh well, I'm allowed to do that now since I won't be on the streets." Big Daddy made the girls keep their weight low. "The customers don't want no fat behinds," he would scold his girls whenever he saw them eating junk or fatty foods. Big Daddy did all the bad eating for his girls, which was evident by his 332lb frame. When she finished eating, Summer washed out her plate and put it away. She then went to the front room to join Mrs. Robertson who was now awake from her nap. The ladies sat and chitchatted while they watched "The Price is Right" on television. After the show was over, Summer excused herself to go and put her belongings in order. When she got back to her room, she began to organize her stuff the best she could in the moderate-sized space. When she finally finished, she sat on the bed and thought about Tess, hoping that she was okay. They were just down the street from each other, but she couldn't even see or talk to her for the time being.

14

Five days had passed since Summer last left the house. She arose very early this morning, she was worried about Tess. Summer decided that she would take a walk to the park and sit in a position where she could watch any activity going on at the house since the park was just a block across from the house. Shortly after she started stirring around the room, Mrs. Robertson lightly tapped on the door. Summer opened the door to see Mrs. Robertson standing there with Tess standing alongside her. Summer couldn't be happier to finally see Tess, but the look of sadness that was etched in her face stopped Summer from the embrace she was excited to give. Tears were flowing from Tess's eyes.

"He's dead," Tess said through her tears.

"Who's dead?" Summer asked nervously.

"Big Daddy," Tess mouthed and cried even more.

Although she was mad about the events that transpired over the past few days, that was not the news Summer wanted to hear. "Noo," she screamed as she grabbed Tess in a tight embrace, the two crying together.

After their cries subsided, Summer pulled back and asked "How? When?"

"This morning," Tess replied. "The paramedics said it was a heart attack and a stroke. I couldn't wake him up. He must have died in his sleep."

Big Daddy did have health issues due to his overweight stature—diabetes, high blood pressure, and hypertension—but he maintained his health with medicine and an active lifestyle. However, his main problem was that he still liked high fattening foods, and this was something Tess was familiar with since she cooked all his meals. Two days after the beating, Big Daddy made Tess pull herself out of bed to cook him some food. Tess was furious with how he acted out against her and Summer, and she had to put an end to it. Besides, she was tired of working the streets for him, and it was time for a change.

Tess pulled out all the ingredients to make his favorite hearty breakfast, but this time, she cooked it a little differently than normal. She grabbed the Crisco and put a glob of it in the skillet. When it was melted, she added the bacon to the skillet and put the burner on low so that the bacon could cook nice and slow, absorbing as much of the Crisco as it could. When the bacon was done, she added the pork sausage patties to the skillet and allowed them to cook just as slow as the bacon. Once the sausage was cooked, she removed them from the cast iron skillet, and she added more Crisco and watched it melt. As soon as it was completely melted, she added the onions and bell pepper, let them cook a bit, and then added the already seasoned potatoes, cooking them to perfection. Afterwards, she whipped up the eggs.

She added butter to the Crisco, bacon, and sausage greased skillet, then poured in the eggs and cooked them until they were nice and fluffy just the way Big Daddy liked them. She checked the oven to see if the extra buttery buttermilk biscuits were almost done.

Tess grabbed his big man-sized plate, which was almost the size of a tray, and began to pile the eggs, bacon, sausage, hash browns, and biscuits onto it. She poured a large mug of sweet tea she had made a little extra sweet this morning. She added a new additional ingredient for sweetener, pineapple juice, which she learned from a recipe she'd gotten off the Internet. Tess made this meal with as much love she could muster from her battered and bruised body. Big Daddy said he could always taste whether his food was made in love or anger. Tess took extra care in preparing the meal that morning. She placed the tray-sized plate and the big mug of tea on a TV tray and carried it out to Big Daddy. He was surely going to enjoy this high-fat meal. Today, Big Daddy finished his breakfast in record time, faster than any other time previously. He must have really enjoyed it.

Later that evening when he returned home, Tess was finishing up a dinner of fried thick-cut pork chops, fried potatoes, fried okra, buttered beans, and biscuits. Biscuits were Big Daddy's favorite, and he liked them with just about every meal. But this time, Tess made honey-buttered biscuits from another recipe she'd found on the Internet, along with pecan pie for dessert. Over the next couple of days, Tess continued to prepare all of Big Daddy's favorite dishes for breakfast, lunch, and dinner. Each day, a feast of waffles, red velvet chocolate chip pancakes, eggs, bacon, sausage, fried chicken, potatoes, and pork chops was waiting for Big Daddy. He always went home to eat because he hated eating out, and Tess made sure he had enough to eat. She made everything from pot roast, fried fish and shrimp, greens, butter beans, and red beans & rice with sausage to pecan pie, peach cobbler, and butter pecan pound cake.

Tess took extra special care in preparing these meals; she did so with lots of love and extra special ingredients. Tess was cooking all of his favorites. *"Maybe I need to toss her around more often,"* Big Daddy thought to himself one evening while eating the spread that was placed before him. Big Daddy was so excited about eating such feasts that he lapsed in taking his medications for a couple of days. Tess helped with that by moving them out of his sight. Oh, and she also stopped reminding him to take them like she always did. The night before his death, Big Daddy was very lethargic after eating his hearty dinner, and instead of watching the news as he normally did, he went straight to bed without a word to Tess. Tess cleaned the kitchen and thought about how strange it was to not see Big Daddy in his usual spot watching television. She went to the bedroom and found him sleeping, another unusual behavior. Every night before Big Daddy went to bed, he always counted his money, rubber banded it, and put it somewhere Tess didn't know about. Not thinking too much into it, and just being happy that he wasn't hounding and pounding on her, Tess instead used this quiet time to relax.

She went into the bathroom and drew a nice, relaxing bubble bath to sooth her weary joints and mind. About an hour later, Tess emerged from the bathroom refreshed, got in bed, and fell right to sleep. The next morning, she arose bright and early at her normal time to prepare Big Daddy's breakfast. Today she decided to prepare something that she hadn't made in a long time: a breakfast casserole. "He will surely love this," she thought to herself. She turned the oven on to 375º then gathered all the ingredients. They always had everything she needed to make any meal. Because Big Daddy only ate home-cooked meals made with fresh food, their refrigerator, deep freezer, and pantry stayed well stocked. After mixing together eggs, sausage, onions, green peppers, cheese, and biscuit mix, she poured the mixture into the baking dish, put it into the oven, and set the timer for 45 minutes. Tess grabbed her pack of cigarettes and lighter from the counter, and she went out to the back porch to smoke and relax while the casserole baked.

Forty-five minutes later, the oven timer went off signaling the casserole was done. Tess jumped up and rushed into the kitchen to turn the oven off because Big Daddy hated annoying noises; he didn't even use an alarm clock. As she moved about the kitchen preparing his plate, she noticed that it was very quiet in the front room. She peeked her head out of the kitchen to check on Big Daddy, but she didn't see him sitting in his recliner listening to the television and reading the newspaper awaiting his morning meal. Confused, Tess went to the bedroom. She saw that he was still in the same spot and the same position he was in when she left him to go make breakfast. This was not normal. Big Daddy was a very early riser, and he was always up shortly after she arose. Tess went over to him and shook him as she called out his name, but he didn't budge nor move. She continued to do so repeatedly, and when he still didn't move, she panicked. Tess grabbed his wrist to check his pulse and felt none. She dropped his arm, dropped down to her knees, and cried because it appeared that the man who she had been with for the past 16 years was now gone. Gathering herself, she reached into her robe pocket, pulled out her cell phone, and dialed 911.

The paramedics arrived, and she walked them to the bedroom where Big Daddy laid still. They checked him out thoroughly, and then they told her that it looked like he suffered both a heart attack and a stroke in his sleep. Upon hearing this, Tess let out a loud cry. Both tears of sadness and joy flowed from her eyes. She was now free.

Three days later, family, friends, acquaintances, customers, and enemies all gathered at the Old St. Paul Catholic Church of Gentilly to pay their respects to the 59-year-old dominance of the small community. Many were sad, but others were glad that Everett Charles "Big Daddy" Claiborne would no longer be controlling the streets. Tess and Summer were both amongst the sad, but they sided more with the glad that Big Daddy would no longer be here to control and torment their lives. Not many good things were said about Big Daddy during the moment of reflections other than how people were thankful that he gave out free turkeys for Thanksgiving, gave free hams for both Easter and Christmas, and held a Community Easter egg hunt for the kids. Following the service, the body was laid to rest in a nearby cemetery, and everyone gathered back at the church for the repast. Afterwards, everyone returned to their normal lives, except for Tess and Summer. They both would now be able to live new, normal lives.

The ladies went back to the house and sat solemnly on the couch until they both fell asleep from the exhaustion of the day's activities. Tess awoke first then she woke Summer up. She told Summer to follow her to the bedroom that she shared with Big Daddy. Once in the bedroom, Tess went into the closet and drug out a big, heavy chest. She then grabbed Big Daddy's keys to search for the right one to open the chest. After all these years, Tess never knew what was in the chest, but now it was time she found out. She tried every key in the lock until the right one finally worked, and the locked popped open. Nervously, Tess looked over to Summer, who nodded her head urging Tess to lift the lid. When she lifted the top, both their eyes grew big at the massive stacks of money stashed inside. They looked at each other with smiles spread across their faces and tears in their eyes.

"So all the money that our bodies have made over the years has been here all along," Tess uttered.

"Looks like it," Summer concurred. Tess and Summer hugged, jumped, and squealed in excitement about the new life that they will be able to create for themselves.

"What do you think about taking some and giving it to the other girls?" Summer asked. "I really would like to see them off the streets."

"Good idea," Tess agreed and begin pulling stacks of money from the chest.

Later, Tess grabbed her phone and texted the other 6 girls that worked for Big Daddy. She told them that she wanted to take them out to dinner tomorrow, and she had something she wanted to give them. She told them to meet her at Landry's Seafood House in the French Quarter at 6pm. She received "ok" responses from each of them, but Tess would need to pick a few of them up because they didn't have cars.

The next evening, Tess and Summer were dressed to the nines to go out for a night on the town. Tess grabbed her Louis Vuitton Neverfull GM bag and put in 6 envelopes filled with $6,000 to give to each girl, which should be enough to get them on their feet. Tess and Summer headed out of the house, jumped into Big Daddy's luxury Buick, and headed to pick up the girls who needed rides to Landry's. When they were all there and seated at a quaint corner table, Tess told the ladies to order whatever they wanted, including drinks, appetizers, entrees, and desserts. The ladies took full advantage of this generous opportunity for a fancy meal, which only came ever so often if a customer wanted to go above and beyond.

During the meal, Tess thanked every lady for their service to Big Daddy's business, and she apologized for any mistreatment they received. Then, Summer spoke up. She told the ladies "I had a life changing experience that has led me to change my life around, and I want to encourage y'all to leave the streets and seek ways to live better, more productive lives."

Tess continued by telling the ladies, "I know that Big Daddy paid you for your services and took care of a lot of your living arrangements and basic needs, but in effort to help y'all get off the street as Summer suggested, we have something for you."

She reached into her bag, pulled out the envelopes, and handed them to each of the ladies. When they opened the envelopes and saw the amount of cash inside, their eyes grew wide. Some expressed their gratitude with tears in their eyes and others were just shocked by such a gesture. The dinner concluded, and each of the ladies hugged Tess and Summer in gratitude and wished one another well.

Days following the funeral and dinner meeting, Summer and Tess went about the house chitchatting and enjoying one another as they packed up Big Daddy's belongings to donate to Goodwill. Suddenly, Tess got quiet and asked Summer in a soft voice, "How does it feel to be saved?" This is something that had been weighing heavily on Tess's mind ever since Summer revealed this to Big Daddy.

Summer responded, "Well, I really don't know. I can tell there's something different about me, but I really don't know how to explain it." Then, Summer told Tess about the information she found on the Internet about what it meant to be saved, which is why she felt like she couldn't go back out on the street. Tess said, "I wonder if I should get saved. Or is it too late?" Summer came up with a suggestion, which Tess thought was a good idea, and the two squealed in excitement. Things were starting to look up for them.

15

Tess and Summer put their overnight bags in the trunk of Big Daddy's car. Tess got in on the driver's side and Summer on the passenger side. This was going to be their first road trip, girl's fun day, and they were both excited. After all the time they'd been living together, they had never done anything for fun except go shopping. Big Daddy was all about business, so all they ever did was work. Tess had never been out of New Orleans, so she was super excited to finally be going somewhere outside of Louisiana. Summer was only a little thrilled to take Tess to see the place where she'd run away from, twice. Although it was a major source of pain for her, thanks to meeting Melinda, it was now the source of change since the pain wasn't there anymore. Yes, she still had some memories, but the pain associated with those memories seemed to have dissipated. They talked the entire time during the 3-hour ride. The conversation was lively, upbeat, and void of the dread or sadness of their previous conversations. The death of Big Daddy brought some light back to their lives, and for that, they were thankful and happy.

The ladies arrived in Natchez at 1pm on a hot spring afternoon. Since they hadn't had anything to eat, they were ready for a meal. Summer was anxious for Tess to meet Melinda, despite her first encounters with the lady. She directed her to the *Eat in Route* diner, and they pulled into the parking lot and parked. They sat in the car, looked at one another, and then quietly stared straight ahead at the building.

"Well, let's do this," Summer said breaking the silence.

"Let's do this," Tess responded, her stomach tied in knots from her nerves.

The two emerged from the car dressed alike in blue jean shorts, white T-shirts that read FREE, and white converse sneakers. They grabbed their Louis Vuitton handbags and headed toward the diner. When they entered, the hostess greeted the ladies and asked for the number in their party in which they replied, "Two." The hostess asked them to wait as she went and prepared their table. While they waited to be seated, Summer glanced around the diner to see if she spotted Melinda.

The hostess returned and guided the ladies to a booth to be seated. As they perused the menu, an older gentleman came to the booth, introduced himself as Evan, and asked for their drink orders. Tess ordered iced tea, and Summer ordered a Coke. When Evan returned with their drinks, they placed their food order. Tess ordered the grilled salmon salad, and Summer ordered a double bacon cheeseburger with mustard, lettuce, tomatoes, onions, and fries. Tess looked at Summer with a confused look when she heard what she ordered. "I can eat what I want now," Summer responded to Tess's scolding look. They both burst out laughing. Tess told the waiter she changed her mind and ordered a grilled chicken club sandwich, onion rings, and a root beer soda. When Evan left their table, they burst out into another round of laughter.

They were having small talk when an older lady walked up to their booth. "Baby, I thought that was you," the old lady said looking in Summer's direction. "I have been praying for you, and I am so overjoyed to see that you have returned." At first, Summer was a little dumbfounded as to who the old lady was. Then it finally clicked. She was the woman who at first harassed then calmed and coerced her into the meeting the night she got saved. The old lady just stood there smiling from ear to ear.

"Thank you," Summer offered back politely not knowing what else to say.

"I'm Sis. Ruth," the old lady said before turning her attention to Tess "And who do we have here?"

"This is my friend Tess. She's been raising me," Summer responded, confused as to why she volunteered that last bit of information.

"Pleased to meet you beautiful," Sis. Ruth stated. "You will receive exactly what you came here for." Tess looked at the lady befuddled wondering how she knew she came there looking for something.

"Just trust me baby," Sis. Ruth responded to Tess's thoughts. "You ladies enjoy your lunch," Sis. Ruth shot out as she walked off.

Before Tess and Summer could say anything, the waiter Evan came to their table with their food. The ladies dug right into their delicious looking dishes because they were starving. As she ate her food, Summer kept looking around the diner to see if she could see Melinda, but she hadn't spotted her anywhere. When Evan came back to the table to check on them, she asked him if Melinda was in, but he informed her that Melinda was out of town. Hearing this deflated Summer, especially since she'd brought Tess here to Natchez to meet Melinda so that she could get saved. As he was clearing their empty dishes, Evan asked the ladies if they would like dessert. They both looked at each other and smiled. Tess ordered a slice of carrot cake, and Summer asked for a slice of the triple chocolate cake with a side of vanilla ice cream. Tess said to Summer, "You are really doing it up eating what you want." Summer just smiled and nodded as her mind was preoccupied with the news of Melinda not being in town. When Evan walked away from the table, Sis. Ruth walked up and occupied the space he'd just vacated. She was a very caring and gentle old lady, but she was always showing up without being beckoned.

"How long will you ladies be in town?" she asked.

"We were planning to stay to a couple of days," Summer started, "But since we came to see Melinda and she is not in town, we will just go ahead and leave."

"You will do no such thing," Sis. Ruth replied. "Let me invite you ladies to come visit with me and stay as long as you like. I have plenty of room." Summer and Tess stared at each other then hesitantly shrugged their shoulders as if to say *it couldn't hurt*.

The waiter brought back their cakes, and they asked him to pack them to-go and bring the check. Evan left and quickly returned. As he was handing the ladies their to-go packages and check, Sis. Ruth politely took the check from him.

"I'll take care of this."

"Oh no, we can't let you do that," Tess insisted.

But Sis. Ruth wasn't hearing that, and she walked toward the cashier. The baffled ladies trailed closely behind her after leaving a $20 tip on the table. Sis. Ruth paid the two checks then instructed the ladies to follow her. When they got outside to the parking lot, she pointed out her car to them. They got into their car, and when Sis. Ruth pulled out, they proceeded to follow. After about a 5-mile drive, they arrived to an older neighborhood, and as they drove through the streets, Summer started to get an eerie feeling. She looked left and right again and again at the small old houses. The surrounding area started to look familiar.

"I think this is the neighborhood I grew up in," Summer whispered.

"Uh oh," Tess gasped. "Do you want to leave?"

"I don't know," Summer responded. Tess continued to drive behind Sis. Ruth until she put on her left signal to turn into the driveway of a baby blue house with yellow trim. It was a well-kept looking home with a well-landscaped lawn.

"Wait. She lives on this street?" Summer blurted out in a panic. "That means she must know me." Summer got really nervous and started to sweat. "I think this is a set-up," she said, anger rising in her.

"Calm down sweetie. We don't know what's going on yet," Tess said in a soothing tone.

"No, no, let's get out of here. I have to get away from here. I don't know what she's going to try to do with me," Summer exclaimed.

Bad memories flooded Summer's mind, and she started to have a nervous breakdown. Sis. Ruth was out of her car and standing in the driveway, not understanding why the girls' car was just sitting in the middle of the street. She immediately launched into prayer, praying in the spirit for the power of God to take over. But the car just sat there. As she looked at it, it looked like something was going on with Summer. Sis. Ruth prayed more fervently against any satanic attacks as she walked slowly towards the car. Tess saw Sis. Ruth approaching the car and became confused on what to do as Summer was yelling at her to drive off. She didn't want to be rude and disrespect the old lady who had been nothing but pleasant towards them and even paid for their lunch. Tess made the more adult decision to pull over out of the street in front of the house. She opened her door, got out of the car, and stepped to Sis. Ruth.

"Thank you for the invitation, but unfortunately, we won't be able to stay," Tess informed her.

"Tell me what's going on," Sis. Ruth asked gently.

Tess looked at Sis. Ruth, over her shoulder into the car, then back at Sis. Ruth. Sis. Ruth stood patiently waiting for Tess to speak, but she didn't. Patting Tess on the hand while telling her everything was going to be alright, Sis. Ruth moved cautiously over to Summer's side of the car. She carefully reached for the door handle and slowly opened the door. Summer was heaving as if she was having a panic attack. Sis. Ruth placed a gentle hand on her back and softly spoke words of comfort until Summer slowly calmed down. Coming to herself, Summer realized they were pulled over and looked around. Summer thought the old lady was trying to take her back to the house of her youth, which was at the dead end of the block.

Summer never knew of the old lady when she lived there, and she questioned internally if the lady really knew who she was. Sis. Ruth lovingly coerced Summer to get out of the car and come into the house, which she obliged. She hesitantly and nervously walked through the lawn toward the house. Going inside the house, Tess and Summer took a seat on the plastic-covered pink, floral couch in the living room as they were instructed while Sis. Ruth went into the kitchen. The girls looked around the small home, which was very clean, fresh smelling, well decorated, and had an extremely peaceful feeling.

Several moments later, Sis. Ruth came out of the kitchen carrying a tray of lemon butter pound cake and glasses of hot tea. Sis. Ruth always believed that comfort food could calm anybody's weary soul, nerves, or distress. She knew that thick slices of her homemade lemon butter pound cake, which was sold in bakeries, restaurants, and grocery stores all over Mississippi, would do just the trick for Summer. She handed out the plates of cake and cups of tea and told them to enjoy. Everyone sat and ate in silence. All that was heard from the young ladies were moans of pleasure as they savored the moist, mouthwatering, and delectable dessert. "Delicious," they both said to express their gratitude.

"Now baby, tell me what is going on with you?" Sis. Ruth lovingly asked Summer.

Summer sat up even more in her seat, the plastic making a noise under her movement, and told Sis. Ruth, "I grew up on this block and it was a place of hurt, pain, and sorrow for me."

"You are now free from that hurt, pain, and sorrow dear, so you no longer have anything to fear," Sis. Ruth responded. Summer thought about it for a moment then shook her head in agreement. Sis. Ruth asked Summer several questions about which house she lived in and who her parents were.

"I lived in the last house at the dead end on the other side of the street. I am Timmy and Bernie's daughter Summer, and I ran away on my 13th birthday."

Sis. Ruth leaned forward and looked closely at Summer. Feeling a bit uncomfortable, Summer shifted her gaze away from the old lady's visual inspection of her. She couldn't understand why the people in this town, who she'd never seen before, kept looking at her with such intensity. Sis. Ruth finally spoke. She told Summer that she was a part of the prison ministry at her church, which goes to visit the women's prison once a month.

"There is an inmate there whose name is Bernadette, and she mentioned to us when we first started doing ministry there that her oldest daughter ran away on her 13th birthday. She said it devastated her so much because it was her fault."

127

With tears now flowing from her eyes, Summer told Sis. Ruth that was her mother.

She then asked, "My father?"

Sis. Ruth told Summer, "He's in jail as well." Summer let out a sigh of relief, happy that her parents were suffering punishment for their crimes. Sis. Ruth also revealed to Summer that both parents had HIV and her siblings were in foster care.

"Siblings?" Summer said shocked to hear she had siblings.

"Yes, a boy and a girl," Sis. Ruth replied.

Sis. Ruth got up, walked over to Summer, pulled her to standing, and embraced her in a grandmotherly hug. As she held a crying Summer, Sis. Ruth prayed a prayer of comfort and spoke words of encouragement. She held the girl for a long time and let her weep in her arms. Tess sat on the couch and cried for her own pain that she experienced as a child and throughout her entire adult life. Noticing Tess, Sis. Ruth reached her hand out to her, and Tess grabbed her hand and joined them.

Then, Sis. Ruth asked Tess, "Are you ready to receive Jesus?"

Tess cried out a soft "Yes." While praying for Tess, Sis. Ruth had her repeat the confession of salvation. After she completed the prayer, Tess was crying even harder, and Sis. Ruth embraced her until she was free. Free from the demons, darkness, and sins of her life.

It was still early in the day, but the ladies were extremely exhausted from all the crying. They asked Sis. Ruth if she had a place where they could lie down for a nap.

The house had two spare bedrooms, and she led them each to a room of their own.

Sis. Ruth was only used to cooking for one since she lived alone, so she went into the kitchen to see what type of dinner she could prepare for the three of them as the girls rested. Opening the refrigerator and scanning its contents, she pulled out the catfish she had thawing, some collard greens, and eggs. She walked over to the produce basket on the counter and grabbed several potatoes. Then she took down a can of corn from the pantry. Sis. Ruth prepared and cooked dinner as she prayed for her house guests.

Several hours had passed since Sis. Ruth completed a hearty meal of fried catfish, potato salad, collard greens, hot water cornbread, and fresh banana pudding. Sis. Ruth loved to cook for other people. She was a retired cook of 35 years from the Natchez Adams School District where she worked in elementary, middle, and high schools cooking and serving school lunch. She was now head of the hospitality committee at her church where she prepared and oversaw meal preparations for the Pastor and Pastoral staff weekly and for special events.

It was late in the evening before Tess arose and emerged from her guest room. She slept peacefully; the best sleep she's had in years. When she peeked into the living room and didn't see Summer, she went back to the bedrooms and quietly opened the door to the room Summer was in. Tess walked softly over to the bed and slightly shook Summer to wake her. Summer stirred, startled by the touch. After her eyes adjusted from her slumber, she saw that it was Tess and sat up in the bed. The two chatted about the good rest they'd both gotten then got up to go into the living room to join Sis. Ruth, who was watching the news.

Seeing the girls coming towards her, Sis. Ruth gladly arose from her seat to greet them. She then proceeded to the kitchen to warm their plates of food. Sis. Ruth instructed them to have a seat at the dining room table, and they did as they were told. Once the food was warmed, Sis. Ruth brought the plates to the dining room and placed the plates before them on the table. She blessed their food and told them to enjoy. As they ate the hearty meal, she went to the kitchen and returned with two bowls of banana pudding and two glasses of milk. Sis. Ruth believed in feeding God's people both natural food and spiritual food. The ladies cleaned their plates, thanked Sis. Ruth for the splendidly delicious meal, and dug right into their banana pudding, which was rich, creamy, and even more than delicious. They hadn't eaten so well in a very long time. Although Tess did all the cooking for their house, they were not allowed to eat any fattening or fried foods, and desserts were definitely out of the picture. They thoroughly enjoyed the savory meal of what they had been missing for a very long time.

While Tess and Summer were enjoying their dessert, Sis. Ruth talked to them. She told them, "I would be very honored if y'all would be my guests at church service in the morning." Tess and Summer looked at one another bewildered. They hadn't been to church since Christmas last year.

Sis. Ruth told them, "It'll be ok. Y'all have nothing to worry about." They were very nervous, but they nodded their heads yes.

Then Summer spoke up saying, "We don't have anything appropriate to wear to church."

Sis. Ruth sat pondering for a moment then said enthusiastically, "There's a Wal-Mart on the outskirts of town that's open 24 hours. Y'all can go down there and get you something like a nice skirt or pair of pants and a blouse."

Tess and Summer once again looked at each other upon hearing Wal-Mart because they only wore designer clothes. Sensing their hesitation, Sis. Ruth spoke again, "I know you gals used to wearing them fancy designer clothes, but it's not going to hurt your bodies this one time," Summer and Tess burst into laughter and said, "Ok," in agreement. They each went to their guest rooms to grab their handbags and headed out the door. Sis. Ruth had written down directions to the Wal-Mart, but Tess told her that the car had a navigation system so they would be fine. "We just need your address to get back," she told her. They left to oblige the old lady's request to purchase some decent clothes to wear as her guests at church tomorrow.

They found the Wal-Mart with no problems, parked, and went into the store. Summer pulled her Versace sunglasses from her bag and put them on her face because she didn't want to have any more encounters with strangers staring at her. Summer looked around the junior's section; she was petite and wore a size 6 on her 5'4" frame. Since Tess was more mature, she went to the Misses section. Although, she could probably wear something from juniors seeing as though she was only a size 8 at 5'7" and 130lbs.

Even though they were average height and small in size, they were very shapely with nice hips and round behinds.

Summer found some black stretch slacks and a cute bright colored top. She thought the outfit was simple yet cute enough to be seen in. Tess found a modern looking dress, not something she'd generally wear, but it was appropriate enough. They both agreed that the sandals they already had would be sufficient, so they went to the cashier to pay for their selections.

Tess and Summer left the Wal-Mart and followed the navigation system's directions back to Sis. Ruth's house. When they returned, Sis. Ruth gave them towels to wash up and told them the time they'd need to be ready to leave. They all said their goodnights but not before asking for another serving of banana pudding, which she happily obliged. Summer and Tess sat at the table eating the exquisite dessert and talked about their nervousness of going to church on a non-holiday. Neither knew what to expect. When they finished, they cleared the table of the dishes, went into the kitchen, and put them away. Summer was the first to take her shower. When she finished, Tess took hers, then they both retired to the rooms for the evening.

16

The smell of bacon cooking woke Tess. She was all too familiar with the smell because she was always the one up bright and early cooking. She laid in bed for a few moments with a smile of contentment and peace spread across her face. She repeated the words she'd heard spoken by Sis. Ruth often while in her presence, "Thank you Jesus." Tess didn't fully understand what that meant, but she figured it must have meant some form of gratitude since the old lady said it often. She got out of bed and left the room to check on Summer before going to dive into the deliciousness that she knew was awaiting her in the kitchen.

When Tess peeked her head through the door, Summer was sitting up on the edge of the bed. She smiled and said, "Good morning." She arose from the bed and went to join Tess. They locked arms and went to join Sis. Ruth for breakfast.

"Good morning," they said in unison to Sis. Ruth when they approached her.

"Good morning dear hearts" she spoke with joy. "Have a seat and I'll fix your plates."

She piled their plates high with thick buttermilk pancakes, fluffy eggs, bacon, and country sausage patties. She placed butter and syrup on the table along with glasses of fresh squeezed orange juice. Sis. Ruth went back to the kitchen and returned with a plate of homemade iced cinnamon buns. Tess and Summer couldn't wait to dig in.

Looking at the spread before her, Tess said, "You sure you aren't trying to spoil us."

"I know that's right," Summer agreed. Sis. Ruth just sat with a wide grin on her face, then she bowed her head to say a blessing over the food and the girls. When they finished their food, Tess and Summer just sat at the table feeling fat and definitely full.

"Yeah, Sis. Ruth, you are definitely trying to spoil us. Keep feeding us like this, we may never leave," Tess said laughing. They all laughed in unison.

Sis. Ruth said, "Sweetheart, it's always been my job to feed people, with food and with the word."

"Well, you're doing a good job at it," Tess responded. She got up from her seat and went over to give Sis. Ruth an endearing hug.

"Alright ladies, let's start getting ready," Sis. Ruth urged after they'd been sitting at the table far too long. They each rolled out of their chairs, cleared the table, and cleaned the kitchen before going to their perspective rooms to dress for church.

Summer was the last to emerge from her room due to intense nerves. Even though she wouldn't see Melinda and her husband because they were out of town, she was still anxious about going to church. Summer didn't exactly know why she was a ball of nerves. She joined Tess and Sis. Ruth in the kitchen, who was checking on the pot roast she had in the slow cooker. "Let's get going," Sis. Ruth said as she led the way out the house. They got into their own cars. The church was located on what was called the other side of town because it took 20 minutes to get there. Sis. Ruth pulled out of the driveway, and as Tess was turning around to follow, Summer stopped her.

"Wait, don't go yet," Summer spoke, her voice trembling.

"What's wrong sweetheart?" Tess asked alarmed, noticing how shaken Summer was.

"I don't know why, but I'm really nervous about going to this church," Summer told Tess. "Since the waiter told us Melinda was out of town, I know her and husband won't be there, but I have this strange feeling in the pit of my stomach," she continued.

"You'll be okay," Tess said lovingly, caressing her hand. "I promise."

"Okay," Summer responded softly after a long pause, not totally convinced.

Tess backed out of the driveway and pulled behind a waiting Sis. Ruth. After driving for 20 minutes, they arrived to a vast, open area with not much development around it, and they pulled into a large, open parking lot with only a few cars. Before them was a nice, elegant, medium-sized brick edifice. The church was very beautiful on the outside, so one could just imagine what it looked like on the inside.

When they parked, Sis. Ruth told the ladies, "I have to go in early for prayer and to start the preparations for the pastoral staff meal. Y'all are welcomed to come in with me." They told her that they'd just wait in the car until it was time for the 11:00 am service to start.

While sitting in the car, they talked about their nervous feelings on what the service was going to be like since they didn't exactly know what to expect, especially since they'd only been to a Catholic church. Suddenly, they noticed cars started to fill the parking lot in droves. They sat in the car silently watching the church goers emerge from their cars and proceed into the church. They saw some old, some young, families, single people, couples, different races, different ages, and different sizes with some dressed churchy while others dressed casually. When the clock showed 11:00, Tess and Summer looked at each other. A gesture they had been doing quite often during this trip to Natchez. People were still arriving into the parking lot and entering the building.

"Well, I guess it's time to go in," Tess said breaking the silence. Summer looked over at Tess, and without saying a word, she reached for her door handle, opened her door, and slowly slid out of the safety of the car. Summer stood in the open doorway for several seconds before stepping back to close the car door.

As they proceeded towards the building, Summer felt like she was walking through quicksand. Her Giuseppe Zanotti sandaled feet felt heavy with every step she took. After what seemed like they were walking the green mile, they finally reached the entrance, and the door was immediately swung open as they approached. They were greeted with warm smiles and "Welcome to Kingdom Culture Worship Center." The ladies returned the smiles and welcomes and walked through the beautifully decorated and massive glass doors. As they stepped further into the immaculately cream and gold-colored lobby with marble floors, they were greeted again with a warm welcome and a hug. They were asked if they were first time visitors. When they responded, "Yes," to the greeters, they were given a visitor's pack and instructions for completing the guest card before they were directed towards the wood doors leading to the sanctuary.

Upon entering the doors of the sanctuary, they were immediately mesmerized by the beauty of the open and airy light-golden colored sanctuary with burgundy pews. The beauty of this building alone was enough to cause the nerves of anyone to dissipate, and that's exactly what happened to both Tess and Summer. They were greeted by an usher who again welcomed them and ushered them forward for seating. Everyone was standing as a choir up front was singing an upbeat Gospel song. The usher seated them in the first available seats for two towards the middle of the sanctuary on the seventh row. The sanctuary wasn't very large, but it was a nice, intimate size and was already almost completely filled. Tess and Summer were able to sit close to the end of the aisle as others moved down. They stood with the others and watched the choir sing.

After the choir sung three more songs, as the last song ended, a young, light-skinned-lady who was dressed in a very tight black suit with a very loud voice, approached the podium and began speaking. She exhorted the congregation for a few moments before asking everyone to take their seats for the reading of the announcements. When she finished the lengthy announcements, a large, burly man approached the podium to welcome the first time visitors. He asked "If there is anyone here visiting Kingdom Culture Worship Center for the first time, please stand." Once again, Tess and Summer looked at each other. When the man asked again for first time visitors to please stand, they slowly rose from their seats and stood with the others who were already standing. As the choir sung a welcome song, people came over to greet and welcome them to the service.

When the welcome concluded, the man told the congregation that it was time to worship God with their offering. Summer and Tess both reached into their purses and pulled out money. They opted out of completing an envelope and just placed their money in the bucket as it passed. After the offering, the man told the congregation, "The choir will sing another selection, and then the next voice you hear will be that of our Pastor. Please stand as he comes up."

Summer looked over at Tess, her eyes wide. When she heard the word, "Pastor," her heart began to beat fast, matching the beat of the music that the band had started playing. Tess grabbed Summer's hand and gave it a tight squeeze. The song was another up-tempo song about your name being victory. Tess clapped her hands along with everyone else while Summer stood still. The song came to an end as a tall, medium-built man wearing a navy blue suit ascended the steps to the podium. Summer could hardly see his face because of the people standing up in front of her short 5'4" stature.

"Good morning and welcome everyone," the Pastor spoke. "You may take your seats." Everyone sat, but Summer still couldn't see ahead of her because of the big hair lady she was seated behind. The keyboard player was playing softly. The man at the podium started to sing praises to the Lord, then he prayed. Afterwards, he said, "I want to once again welcome our first time visitors. We don't take it lightly that you chose to worship with us today. Would you please stand? Everyone, give them a hand as they stand."

Summer and Tess stood again along with about 10 others. After she stood, Summer was now able to get a clear glimpse of the man's face. When she saw it, she could not believe her eyes. She leaned her body and head forward just a little to get a better look. Her eyes were seeing correctly. Standing before her was the same face that she'd seen on the billboard about a week ago. Her heart began to beat rapidly, her stomach began to turn, her palms turned sweaty, and her armpits started to sweat. Summer's body began to spasm with every word he spoke as his voice boomed through the speakers. With every word he spoke, memories of every whisper, every touch, every kiss, every penetration, and every thrust that he did to her young girl body came back to her.

The flashbacks caused Summer to cry silently at first, and then she screamed out, "No, no, no." People turned toward the screams. Her body shook violently. She couldn't stay in there. She had to get out of there. All of a sudden, Summer bolted out of the row, stepping on people's feet to get out. She darted towards the doors of the sanctuary, threw them open, and ran through the lobby and out the entrance to the parking lot, with Tess close on her heels carrying both their handbags.

Seated on the front row in her reserved seat, Melinda pushed herself up slightly when she heard the screams. She looked towards the direction they were coming from and saw that it was Summer, as did Sis. Ruth. When Summer took off, so did they along with Melinda's armor bearer, the Assistant Pastor, some ushers, and security. When they got outside, Summer was at their car crying loudly and uncontrollably. Melinda approached and reached out to touch Summer, who shoved her hand away yelling, "Don't touch me! You're married to that monster!" Melinda was confused. She had no idea what Summer was talking about. Sis. Ruth stood off to the side praying fervently in the spirit for God to intervene. Melinda tried again to get Summer to calm down asking, "What are you talking about?" but Summer was crying hysterically.

Soon, Pastor Wilburn Thibodeaux, followed by his entourage, showed up outside to see what all the commotion was about. When he saw Summer's face up close, he stopped dead in his tracks. Wil couldn't believe that after all these years, she came back to Natchez and had the gall to show up at his church. This caused an anger to stir in him that soon dissipated as Summer began to yell obscenities at him while calling him a child molester. Everyone around

140

looked on with stunned and shocked faces at how this girl could speak such derogatory things about their Pastor. Wil kept a calm composure while trying to silence Summer by telling her, "You must have me mistaken for someone else."

But Summer kept going on and on. "The last time you molested me was on my 13th birthday, which was why I ran away from Natchez." She was starting to expose the deep, dark secrets of his past that he thought were long buried, never to come up again. But here he was standing face to face with the young girl he violated sexually many years ago.

Melinda stood frozen in shock. Her heart beating rapidly as she listened to Summer repeatedly say her husband molested her as a child. Melinda turned to Wil, and with a shaky voice and tears running down her face asked, "What is Summer talking about Wil? Why is she saying these awful things about you?" This same girl who God had her praying for, who she prayed with and led her to salvation, was accusing her husband, a Pastor, of molestation. Wil stood there toying with his own thoughts and said nothing.

While Melinda was questioning Wil, Tess and Summer jumped in the car, backed away from the crowd, and drove off. With such sadness in her eyes and tears continuing to roll down her face, Melinda asked Wil again, "What is she talking about? Why would she say such horrible things about you?" Still, he didn't respond, and she pleaded with him for an answer. By that time, Charla and her mother had come outside and stood by watching the scene. She didn't see Summer, but she heard Melinda's questioning of Pastor Wil.

"First Lady," she said, "Summer told me the same things too, but I didn't believe her. She said that is why she ran away in New Orleans on our 13th birthday." After hearing that confession from Charla, Pastor Wil's head just dropped as tears began to flow from his eyes. He put his hands to his face and wept. This gesture sent Melinda into a tizzy. She began hitting him, pushing him, and saying, "So it's true!" repeatedly. She called him a monster just as Summer had. Sis. Ruth finally stepped forward and grabbed Melinda in a tight embrace, allowing her to weep sorely on her shoulder.

Pastor Wil turned away from the crowd and walked back towards the church with his head hung low. He went inside the building, but instead of going back into the sanctuary to the pulpit, he went down the hallway that led to his private Pastor's quarters. When he reached his office, he pulled his keys from his pocket and unlocked the door. He stepped inside and locked the beautiful mahogany door behind him. Wil stood inside the expansive office space admiring its beautiful décor of cherry wood furniture, custom burgundy and gold drapes, large bookcases full of books, and the custom burgundy and gold couch with matching chairs in front of his huge custom desk. The office was custom designed by him to match his exquisite taste.

Wil walked over to the kitchen, opened the door of the mini refrigerator, and pulled out a bottle of water. He opened the top and took a long swallow to quench his very dry throat. Wil sat the water bottle down on the counter, walked over to his desk, and plopped down in his oversized custom leather chair with the initials WT embroidered in the headrest. He sat with his elbows propped on the desk and his head in his hands, wrestling back and forth with his thoughts. He could not believe his past had come back to expose him after all these years.

He'd repented to God when he got saved after he heard the news of Summer's disappearance 8 years ago. Two years later, God called him to be a Pastor. He went to seminary school and graduated top of his class. Three years after that, he started a church that has been growing ever since. They just moved into the new church building a year ago. "So, why on earth would God allow this to happen now, at this time?" Wil questioned internally. He and Melinda had just returned last night from a speaking engagement in Arkansas that took place from Thursday night to Saturday morning. They had such an awesome service as the spirit of God moved in the Faith Conference.

Everything was going so well for him, so he figured God must be pleased with the work he was doing in ministry. He was building up people and traveling to other churches to minister. He had a great marriage, thriving businesses, and a growing ministry where people were being healed, delivered, and set free. Not recognizing that this was an attack from the devil, Wil's thoughts couldn't rest on the fact that his reputation in Natchez, the state of Mississippi, and surrounding states would now be ruined. His thriving ministry was going to suffer once more people found out about his past. Wil could not fathom the thoughts that his on-the-top life would now come crumbling down right before his eyes.

Instead of calling out to God to help him in this situation, Wil continued to sit and wrestle with the thoughts that continued to invade his mind. He knew that he should pray. That's what he taught his congregants to do in times of adversity. But that was a principle that he himself did not follow in this moment. Thoughts of defeat continued to bombard his mind. Wil grabbed his keys from the desk. Hands trembling, he found the tiny key that unlocks the small drawer on the right-hand side of the desk. He sat and stared at the contents of the opened drawer for a moment. Then, he reached his hand inside, gripped the black rubber handle of the steel object, and pulled it out. He looked at it for a few minutes then cocked it. Wil pondered for a moment about what he was about to do until he heard knocks at the door. Not wanting to face whoever was on the other side of the door, he put the gun to his head and pulled the trigger.

The people on the other side of the door heard a loud bang coming from inside the office. Pastor Wil's armor bearer frantically pulled the keys from his pocket to open the door while the others yelled at him to hurry. Once he finally got the door open, they rushed inside to see their Pastor slumped over his desk with blood gushing from his head. Melinda ran into the office, saw her husband, and screamed out, "Noooo," before fainting to the floor. Everyone just stood in the office and the doorway in shock that their Pastor had just committed suicide. After seeing the shocking sight before her, Charla backed out of the office in tears. She asked her mother, "Mom, can you please get the twins from children's ministry? There's something I need to do." When her mother agreed, Charla quickly fled the building.

When Melinda came too, the men rushed to help her up, but she shooed them away with her hand. She just laid on the floor in agony, with a new pain in her soul. She never imagined that this would be the destiny of her life: to marry a man with such a horrifying past whose life would end in suicide. Just when she thought her life was free from tragedy, and she was walking in her purpose by helping other women to get free from their past, this happened.

"Why God?" she screamed out loudly. "What do you want from me now? Why do you keep letting tragedy into my life," Melinda cried out. "Please, no more! I can't take anymore!" she pleaded.

Tess and Summer continued their drive out of Natchez back to New Orleans in silence. As Summer slept on the passenger side, Tess pondered the events of the day. Tess was happy that Summer was finally able to confront the demon of her past, and she hoped that now she would be able to live in peace. Since her incident was more than 30 years ago, and she'd already numbed her pain with sex, drugs, and alcohol over the years, Tess felt it was no longer necessary for her to confront John, her molester. As she received her salvation, she asked God to forgive her of her sins, she spoke aloud her forgiveness of John, and she asked

God to forgive him as well as she was instructed by Sis. Ruth.

Summer had awakened, startled by the ringing of her phone. She grabbed it from her purse and looked at it groggily. Although she did not recognize the number, a Mississippi area code, she answered anyway.

"Hello," Summer answered puzzled.

"Hello Summer, it's Charla," the caller responded. The phone went silent.

When Charla rushed from the church, she made a mad dash to her job at Best Western. She ran inside the hotel, went into the office, and frantically looked through the guest cards to find the one Summer completed while checking in the hotel. When she found it, she quickly scribbled Summer's number on a Post-it, put the files away, and left the office as quickly as she came. Charla sat in her car nervous about the phone call she needed to make. She stared at the number for a few minutes before nervously pressing each number on her phone's keypad with shaky hands.

Charla looked at the phone to check if the call had been disconnected. Seeing that the call was still connected, she said, "Hello?" breaking the silence after not receiving a response from Summer.

"Yes," Summer said firmly.

"I want to apologize for not believing you," Charla said crying. "Will you please forgive me?" Once again Charla received no response from Summer.

Speaking up again, Charla said, "He's gone. He committed suicide in his church office."

"What? Suicide!" Summer finally responded. Tess looked over at Summer when she heard the word suicide.

"Yes, we heard the gun go off, and when they got the door open, we saw him in his office with a gunshot to the head." Charla explained.

"No! He had no right to do that!" Summer shouted angrily. "He didn't even apologize to me for what he'd done to me," she said.

"That coward bastard!" Summer yelled after a long pause.

"I understand, and I know you're hurting. Although he's gone, you still need to release him and forgive," Charla calmly tried to minister to Summer.

"Forgive!" Summer shouted. "I'll never forgive him!"

"Summer, you cannot live your life holding this against him. It'll do you more harm than good. You'll have to let it go," Charla continued.

Summer was silent for a longtime, and Charla heard someone speaking in the background. After several rejections to Tess and Charla's pleas for Summer to forgive, she finally surrendered. "You're right. I do need to live my new life in freedom. He's gone now and that's exactly what I wanted." Summer said matter-of-factly. Following another long moment of silence, Summer whispered, through a fresh set of tears, "I forgive him."

As Summer said those three words, the heavy weight of the day was lifted, and the pressure in her heart immediately disappeared as she slowly exhaled. Tess looked over at Summer from the driver's seat and said, "I'm proud of you." Charla was on the other end of the phone crying tears of joy at the bold step her friend had taken.

"Summer, I'm proud of you. You won't regret the decision you just made." After a short pause, Charla told Summer, "I really do miss you."

"Thank you. I miss you too." Summer spoke softly.

"You take care of yourself, and I do hope to see you again soon. Love you."

"We'll see," Summer responded before ending the call.

Tess and Summer looked at each other with smiles on their faces and tears of joy flowing from their eyes. They continued their return to New Orleans with renewed spirits and a newfound peace and freedom.

Here's an excerpt from Wendi Hayman's debut non-fiction
book
Blind Ambition
Coming Spring 2017
To order email glorytoglorypublications@gmail.com or visit
www.wendihayman.com

Blind Ambition

Intro

I'd heard that rap artists, music producers, record
company execs, or personnel frequented strip clubs all the
time. As I mounted the stage at *Fantasy*, my first night there,
I did so with a goal and one goal only: to be discovered. The
beat dropped, and Ginuwine's *Pony* blared through the
club's speakers. I nervously danced around the pole and
onto other areas of the stage. I continued to dance
seductively as "If you're horny let's do it" rang out, then I
dropped down in a squat position as "ride it, my pony"
followed. I danced the best I could through my nervousness.
As the music continued, dancing around the stage, I tugged
at the stings tied around my neck, and my top fell down
suddenly. I just let it hang in that position because I was too
nervous, shamed, and embarrassed to take it off any further.
As the song neared its end and men stood at the bottom of
the stage, money in hand, I knew they wanted more. I had to
give more. *Fantasy* was after all an all-nude strip club. I had

to give them the fantasy that they came for and would ultimately pay for.

My focus was not on the men or their money. I loved to dance, and I was a darn good dancer. The music videos and award shows I watched growing up had me wanting nothing more than to be dancing background for a rapper. But how did I end up here, on a stage, dancing in the nude? I was a hip-hop dancer, and that was what I was working towards. I knew all the latest hip-hop songs and all the latest and greatest hip-hop dance moves. Nonetheless, there I stood on stage in 6" heels, minus the pink mesh G-string and bikini top that I had on when I first got there, twirling around a pole while men threw money at me. I watched it all fall onto the stage as I continued to dance.

The Decoy Discovery

*God even had a **purpose** for a harlot. Rahab was used to hide the spies sent out by Joshua to view the land in which God promised the children of Israel and she received the favor of the Lord for her and her household. (Joshua 2:1, 12-14)*

When I was around age 8 or 9, I discovered I had a natural talent for dancing. Whenever I heard music, I would just dance. At first, I played my mom's old albums and made up dance steps to the music. Years later, I received a radio as a Christmas gift, and from then on, all I would do is listen to the radio and make up dance routines; I loved to dance and was very passionate about it. One thing that my cousin in Louisiana and I had in common was that she also liked to dance. She and I would go to parties, the skating rink, and although we weren't old enough, the clubs. We did a lot of dancing together in our teenage years. We reaped much attention and unbeknownst to me, a seed had been planted, and I developed a mindset and need for attention, that was the beginning of my straying from my life's purpose.

When I was in elementary school, my parents sent me to a magnet (specialty) school outside of my local neighborhood, where I enrolled in band. I really didn't want to be in band, so I selected what I thought would be an easy instrument to play, the flute, which turned out not be so easy after all. Moving on to middle school, I had to pick two electives, so I selected dance as my first choice. Unfortunate for me, I had to audition and did not get selected because I had no prior dance training. I was forced back into band, and this time I had to put more effort into learning the music. When it was time for me to move into High School, I begged my parents to allow me to go to a school that had a cosmetology program. I enjoyed doing hair and this was also something that my favorite cousin did as well. As I said, I wanted to be just like her. My parents said no and told me that I had to attend a school that had an honors program or that offered advanced college preparatory classes. This worked out well since I went on to graduate in the top 10% and #15 of my class.

I found a high school back in my local neighborhood that was also well known for their band. I was excited to join band in high school because I had been to football games, and I saw during half-time how the band would play popular songs, perform dances, and get the crowd hyped. Unfortunately, things didn't go as I expected. During my freshman year, our school got a new band director, and he was firmly against the half-time dance. As a matter of fact, he did not even allow us to play popular songs in which bands were known to play at football games. My freshman year of high school band was disastrous and not as exciting as I thought it would be. However, because I became pregnant after my first semester, I couldn't remain at public high school anyway and my parents sent me away to live at an adoption agency home because their plan was for me to give the baby up for adoption. However, my aunt stepped in and raised my daughter so that she could remain in the family. It was a blessing that she stayed in the family and that I was able to remain in her life.

Sophomore year, I then transferred to a school closer to home, and I started playing with the band in the summer. I was now excited to be in high school band. The drum majors were very talented and the band dances were the best. I really wanted to be a part of the band, but I didn't want to play an instrument. The dance team wasn't any good, so I didn't want to join them. So I auditioned to be a twirler mainly because I liked the skimpy outfits; however, I didn't make the team, so I was stuck playing an instrument. During practice, I initially had a hard time learning the music, but that didn't bother me because I quickly learned the choreography of the band dance. Dancing was my passion, and I gave it my all at every practice, football game, parade, band competition and school dances. I proved my dance skills and swiftly garnered the attention of male band members and eventually others. I enjoyed the attention and praise that I received from others. I made sure to give maximum effort with every opportunity I was given to dance. Dance became my life, and the attention became my fuel, so I worked hard to excel in band especially the dance portion of performances. I had evolved into a pretty good flute player as well, remaining between first, second, or third chair during my band tenure.

I remained in band only throughout my junior year. Even though I was no longer in band, I still hung out with my band mates, attended band activities and events, and continued traveling with them to parades and competitions. Second semester of my junior year, I enrolled into my high school's Office Education program in which I was fortunate enough to secure my very first job at the NASA Johnson Space Center. I started work at NASA during the summer prior to my senior year and throughout.

When our class took our senior trip to Orlando, FL for a week, our last stop was to Daytona Beach. While on the beach, some friends and I were approached to enter a dance contest called the "Swatch Watch Dance Contest." We decided to enter and join the fun, and we had an exciting time dancing against one another and strangers. There were multiple rounds where someone would get eliminated each round, and I made it through each round until I was 1 of the 2 people in the final round. I won 1st place in the dance contest, and I won a Swatch watch as the prize. That's how good I was at dancing and I was just a high school student competing against college-age and older adults.

After I graduated high school and at the end of my term at NASA, I was offered a full-time position with the opportunity to go to college locally, but I declined and chose to go away to college instead. This was the first regretful mistake I made in life where I strongly believe would have saved me from the journey that I later embarked upon.

In preparing for college, I was eager to become a part of a college band. I had witnessed some performances at college football games I attended. College bands were on another level and performed on a grander scale than high school, so going to college was going to be great, or so I thought. Unfortunately, I allowed my parents to influence my college career path, and I chose pharmacy as a major. I decided to go to Xavier University of New Orleans because they had a top pharmacy program, but the school did not have a band. What the school did have was parties and lots of them. I learned this during freshman orientation. Matter of fact, at the end of the freshmen orientation, the DJ put on music and the MC urged us to come out to the gym floor and dance. At first, I was afraid to because I was in a new environment, but not one to miss an opportunity to dance, I made my way to the dance floor and quickly made my mark. I became known as the freshman girl from Houston who could dance, and as a result, I quickly had college party buddies. Even better, New Orleans was party central with all the college parties, all-nighter parties, Mardi Gras parades and parties, house parties, and the famous French Quarter, and I took part in all of them. I spent my first semester of college, attending more parties then I did studying.

Many college students party to drink, but I partied to dance; I did not drink because dancing was my drink and my drug. While attending these parties, I discovered a popular local dance referred to as the *p-pop*, a dance similar to twerking. When I first saw this dance, I was determined to learn it. Practicing in my dorm room every opportunity I got, I not only learned the dance, I perfected it. I had perfected the dance so well, that while at parties whenever I did the *p-pop*, people thought I was a native of New Orleans.

My first semester grades reflected exactly how much I partied and didn't study, so my mom threatened to make me come back home if I didn't improve my grades the next semester. I quickly found a balance between studying and partying because there was no way that I was going to give up the freedom I had gained while being away in college. In high school, the band was an outlet for me because my mom was mean, strict and would not always allow me to go to the school dances or parties. Most of my high school social life was stifled by always having to babysit my younger sister. So, I was definitely not willing to risk my freedom to go back home.

My Self-Proclaimed Purpose

"But seek first the kingdom of God and His righteousness..."
Matthew 6:33

We didn't have cable television growing up; in fact, my mother still doesn't have it to this day. Visits to relative's homes gave me glimpses of what cable television had to offer. I remember when I was around 15 and I saw my first rap videos and a BET award show. I was so excited to see the background dancers, and this led me to make a self-proclaimed purpose. I declared that I wanted to be a background dancer. I thought that if I became a background dancer, and danced at concerts, in rap videos, and on award shows, then maybe I would have the attention from people that I longed for. I would no longer feel lonely, rejected, or abandoned.

During my second semester in college, I had the opportunity to attend a Greek step show and party at LSU's campus. As soon as the party started, I found my favorite place on the dance floor. If I didn't have anyone to dance with, I would always just go out to the dance floor and start dancing alone. Then it would happen: the attention would be drawn to me and a circle would begin to form around me as I was dancing. This generally happened to me every time I danced at parties and clubs. After the circle formed, different guys would come in to dance with me or dance against me in a challenge, but I would always be able to hold my own. My dancing at this party gained the attention of a local rapper who was in attendance. During a conversation with him, he told me that he was looking for backup dancers; this was music to my ears. Remember, I stated my self-proclaimed purpose was to be a background dancer for a rapper. He and I exchanged information, and he also asked if I'd be able to recruit other girls from campus who would also be interested in auditioning. I was elated to finally get my chance to dance for a rapper.

Several weeks later, I went to audition for the rapper *Quiet Storm* and his manager, and I was selected on the spot. I was immediately thrusted into the rap industry because *Quiet Storm* was an up and coming New Orleans rapper. We began studio recordings, practice sessions, concerts, attending hip hop industry conferences, and eventually he and I became a couple. My freshman year ended, but I remained in New Orleans for the summer to retake a failed class and to work on campus. I continued my relationship with *Quiet Storm* as his girlfriend and dancer. However, due to an issue with my roommate in our off-campus apartment and my inability to afford one on my own, my mom decided it was best that I return to Houston. This was devastating to me, or so I thought. Returning to Houston was actually a set-up on another road that would lead me closer to my *self-proclaimed* purpose.

One Hot Summer